Ignite

Ignite

THE WILDWOOD SERIES

KAREN ERICKSON

AVONIMPULSE

An Imprint of HarperCollinsPublishers

Excerpt from *Smolder* copyright © 2016 Karen Erickson.
Excerpt from *Hard Ever After* copyright © 2016 by Laura Kaye.
Excerpt from *Wild at Heart* copyright © 2016 by Tina Klinesmith.
Excerpt from *The Bride Wore Starlight* copyright © 2016 by Lizbeth Selvig.

EPub Edition MARCH 2016 ISBN: 9780062441188

Print Edition ISBN: 9780062441195

Avon, Avon Impulse, and the Avon Impulse logo are trademarks of HarperCollins Publishers.

AM 10 9 8 7 6 5 4 3 2 1

Chapter One

She wasn't aware they currently shared the same air.

Weston Gallagher stood in the back of the store, partially hidden by a towering display of Coke products. The beginning of summer meant every end cap in the supermarket was pushing snacks, beer, and soda. West had had no idea an endless stack of vivid red twelve-packs would make a damn good hiding place.

He also hadn't planned on hiding in plain sight. He was a grown-ass man. If he wanted to pass by Harper Hill like she didn't exist, he could. But he wasn't that mean. She *did* exist. And damn she looked good.

Really good. Better than he remembered.

No one noticed him hovering on the other side of the stacks of Coke, peeking around them at the pretty woman oblivious to his presence. Most of the locals—the people he grew up with, the ones who'd known him since he'd toddled around in diapers and a dirty face—didn't shop at the fancy new grocery store on the outskirts of town. That was for the deluge of tourists who invaded his hometown every summer. Eager to spend their hard-earned dollars on expensive groceries they could stock their rented cabins with, his mom had told him bitterly last time he talked to her on the phone.

All the locals loved to mock the tourists, but never too hard. They were the ones who kept the money streaming in most of the year.

Considering he sort of felt like a tourist since it had been years since he last set foot in Wildwood, he thought he'd avoid the reunion show that his appearance at Gus's Grocery would generate. That's why he was shopping in such a generic location. So to see someone he knew—rather intimately, he might add—was shocking.

His hiding spot did have one advantage. It allowed him ample time to check Harper out. He hadn't seen her in years beyond the occasional photo on social media—they weren't friends on Facebook or anything crazy like that, but they did share a lot of mutual friends.

Like his younger sister, Wren, otherwise known as Harper's *best* friend. Harper had been a part of his life for…most of his life. He remembered her as a little girl who knew how to work a trembling lower lip like nobody's business. He remembered Harper as an awkward preteen with braces and a constant red zit on her chin. Then somehow, someway, she'd blossomed into this beautiful, curvy, sweet girl who always looked at him like she wanted to worship at his feet and gobble him up, all at the same time.

Scrubbing a hand over his face, West glanced down, trying to blot memories of Harper out of his brain by staring at the contents of his shopping cart instead. Beer. Ground beef for burgers since he was having his brothers over for dinner tonight. Chips. Cereal. Milk. Just the necessities for now. He was scheduled for work in two days and he'd be eating at the station most of the time anyway. If he was lucky and the season was extra busy, he'd get a lot of overtime and rarely be home.

Yeah, being a firefighter meant a season full of endless fires was a "good" fire season—financially only, of course. He wasn't a fan of seeing death and destruction caused by a raging fire, but he did appreciate the adrenaline rush that filled him every time they loaded up the engine and took off to a call. Though now *he* was the one driving the engine, thanks to his promotion.

That's why he was home. He'd gotten promoted and moved to a new ranger unit and station. He was back in Wildwood, ready to prove that he wasn't Weston Gallagher, King Troublemaker anymore. He'd changed his wicked ways. He was solid; a hard worker, following in his father's footsteps and ready to prove every single one of the residents wrong. He knew how they felt about him. How he'd left Wildwood with his proverbial tail tucked between his legs.

Well, no more. He was dependable. People could count on him. When he was younger, he never wanted that. It had felt like more responsibility than he couldn't handle. He'd make a lot of mistakes then. He wanted to correct them.

Badly.

"Weston Gallagher? Is that really you?"

His spine stiffened at the sound of a familiar feminine voice coming from behind. Slowly he turned, hoping that Harper had snuck up behind him, though he knew deep down the voice didn't sound like Harper's. Still, he had high hopes. His heart was racing. His palms were sweaty.

Disappointment crashed over him mixed with the tiniest bit of relief. It wasn't Harper but Delilah Moore, his ex-girlfriend from high school.

"I thought that was you!" Delilah rushed toward him, enveloping him in a warm hug. "Lane mentioned you were moving back this weekend."

West frowned as he withdrew from her arms. Delilah talked to his big brother? Since when? "*Lane* told you?"

Her cheeks went a little pink as she nodded. "Everyone talks to Lane, West. He's always out patrolling around, you know? Our public hero and all that jazz."

West grimaced. His big brother could never do any wrong. Lane Gallagher was the oldest child and the perfect one of the Gallagher clan. The guy everyone looked up to, including West himself. He'd idolized his older brother…until he didn't.

The constant comparisons had become too much. Too difficult to deal with, especially when everything went sideways. West had discovered it was a lot more fun to screw around and get in trouble than be good like Lane.

At one point during their teen years, Delilah had been his accomplice in getting into trouble. They'd had good times. Reckless and a little wild, though he'd always been the one who pushed her. But she soon tired of it. Tired of him.

He couldn't blame her.

"Why are you here at the fancy supermarket, Dee?" He noticed her look of irritation at his using her old nickname, but that didn't faze him. She'd get over it. They'd known each other long enough that he was sure she couldn't stay irritated with him for too long.

"It's the only place that has this particular brand of energy bars I like." She held her shopping basket up. It was loaded with boxes and boxes of energy bars, all the same brand, but in a variety of flavors.

West frowned, quickly glancing over his shoulder to see if he could spot Harper. She was still standing by the frozen food section. "Why so many? You live on those things or what?" She'd never had to watch her figure from what he remembered. She was naturally slender and had danced her ass off most of her life.

"I need them for my students—we sell them along with other nutritious snacks that'll give them fuel, not turn them sluggish." At his confused look she continued. "I own the dance studio now. I bought it from Miss Lesandre a few years ago," she said proudly, smiling at him.

"No shit?" He rubbed his chin, looking over his shoulder again. Harper had just been at the frozen foods section only moments ago and now she wasn't. Where'd she go?

"Yeah. It's been hard work but so rewarding. If you can't make a living as a professional dancer, you may as well teach it, right? Though some of it's a challenge. Like keeping the books." She rolled her eyes. "I'm not so good with the business side. That's where your sister comes in."

"Wren?" His only sister had been born into a sea of brothers—three of them to be exact. And now she worked at a dance studio? How did he not know this? Granted, he hadn't talked to her in a while. And by talk he meant text, since that was how he and Wren communicated lately, if at all. "What does she do there?"

She couldn't be teaching classes because she'd never taken dance lessons a day in her life. She was too busy trying to keep up with her brothers to be bothered with girly stuff like ballet.

"She's my business partner. It only happened a few months ago, but I'm so glad to have her help. I really needed it, and now we're both invested in the business." Delilah beamed, her eyes dancing with mischief. "Harper! Look who I just found."

West's heart bottomed out at the sound of her name, at the fact that she would know he was there. He kept his panicked gaze on Delilah a moment too long and her eyebrows drew together, like she had no idea what the problem could be.

Of course, she wouldn't know. No one knew that once upon a time, many years ago, on a late summer night under a star-filled sky, he'd kissed Harper Hill for hours. Hours and hours. Long, tongue-filled kisses that had induced wandering hands and sighs full of longing. Oh, and the biggest case of blue balls West had ever endured in his life. That hours-long kissing session had been worth it though. Harper Hill had tasted just as good as he'd imagined. She'd melted in his arms, so responsive, so damn sweet…

And then he'd walked away like a complete jackass, never contacting her again. All along he'd known he was leaving. He'd completed two seasons at the Wildwood fire station straight out of high school. Put in for a promotion wherever he could, letting the lady in human resources know that he wanted the hell out of the ranger unit. Far away from his hometown, far away from his family, specifically his dad, so he could start fresh. He'd kissed Harper that night because he could. Because he desperately wanted to. Because he knew he wouldn't have to face the consequences of his actions.

He'd moved out of Wildwood the next day and never looked back.

Not one of his finer moments. Did Wren know about his make-out session with Harper? Best friends shared everything, but he had a feeling Harper had never confided in hers about the two of them making out. After all, he was Wren's big brother. At the time, Harper had been off-limits. Forbidden.

She still was. So much that he could hardly chance a look at her.

But he had to. Look. Just to see if she was as pretty as she'd been from far away when he'd lurked behind Coke boxes and stared at her.

Very slowly, very carefully, trying his best to keep his smile in place, he turned his head and met Harper's gaze for the first time in what felt like forever.

His knees felt a little wobbly.

Harper was even more beautiful up close. Long hair the color of the sun riding low in the sky, reds and golden browns and strands of blonde that waved past her slim shoulders, with that cute little pert nose sprinkled with freckles. Freckles she'd always hated.

That one night, his last in his hometown, he'd done his damnedest to kiss every single one.

Her dark brown eyes flashed at him, and those perfect, delicious, bee-stung lips didn't slide up in that natural sunny smile of hers. Harper Hill was friendly. Beyond friendly. The entire Hill family had a reputation to uphold in this town, and Harper was just as cheerful as all the rest of them. She had a natural way about her, drawing people in, always surrounded by friends—by people who wanted to be her friend, like it was a privilege to bask in her glory.

Right now though, she looked like she wanted to draw and quarter West. Maybe hang him up by his toes so he dangled above the ground, much like he remembered his dad and grandpa doing when they brought home a buck during hunting season.

Yeah. He'd never been one for blood sport as a kid or an adult. Harper though?

She appeared ready to shoot him dead with just the look in her pretty brown eyes.

IT TOOK EVERYTHING within Harper Hill to draw herself up to her full height of a mighty five-foot-three and appear indifferent. Inside, she quivered like a leaf. After all, Weston Gallagher stood in front of her in the flesh, all six feet plus of him. And he looked so good, so ridiculously sexy, her stomach fluttered at the way he smiled at her all friendly like. As if the last time they'd seen each other they hadn't had their tongues down each other's throats. Or their hands all over each other's bodies.

She felt her cheeks warm remembering all the places West had touched her.

"Hey, Harper," he said, his voice deep and sure. She'd never forgotten the sound of his lazy drawl. How it seemed to ooze over her like warm, thick honey, making her languid and weak.

So weak.

Not right now though. Nope, right now hearing him say her name, looking at her like they were old friends, maybe even mere acquaintances, made fire flash in her blood, setting its temperature to boiling.

"Weston Gallagher. I heard a bad rumor you were coming back to town," Harper sniffed, offering him her best fake smile. The one she didn't use very often because damn it, she was a *nice* person. Everyone said so. "Looks like it was true."

Delilah gaped at her, her big brown eyes wide with disbelief. Harper was never unfriendly to anyone. Nice had been bred down into the very essence of her. The entire Hill family, since her great-grandparents moved to Wildwood ages ago, were known as the friendliest people in town. Wildwood's own homegrown Welcome Wagon, not that anyone knew what a Welcome Wagon was anymore.

Harper did. She was queen of the Welcome Wagon now. Gracious and kind and, above all, accommodating.

Except when it came to Weston Gallagher.

"Good to see you, too, Harper. As always." He gave her a salute, his smile actually growing into a full-blown grin, the cocky bastard. "You're even prettier than I remembered."

And with that, he turned tail, taking his cart along with him as he got the hell out of there.

Fast.

"He didn't even say good-bye," Delilah grumped, sending Harper a look that was full of way too many questions. "What was that all about, girlfriend?"

Harper tilted her nose in the air. "I have no idea what you're talking about." Inside she still quaked with nerves. She'd seen West for the first time in years and hadn't fallen apart. Hadn't thrown herself at him either.

That was the best part. The part she'd worried about most of all. This had been some sort of test, running into him at the too-expensive supermarket in town. Besides, who shopped here? No one she knew.

"What are you doing here anyway?" she asked Delilah, spotting the reason as soon as she peeked inside the basket hanging from her arm. "Oh. The power bars."

She was known as the health nut dance instructor around town, but everyone adored Delilah. What was not to adore? She was beautiful and spirited and moved with a natural grace that Harper could only hope to emulate. She'd taken dance with Delilah a long time ago, when they were little girls in matching black leotards and pale pink tights.

But that was years ago. Harper had never taken well to dance. Too awkward, too clumsy, too short. And she'd lost any glimmer of grace she'd picked up in ballet—not that it had been much.

"They're the best on the market. But so expensive." Delilah shook her head. "Why are you here?"

"They have Grandma's favorite brand of coffee." She gestured toward the cart, which was filled with two freshly ground bags of coffee and a few other items. "I have a feeling if I laid her out on an operating table and cut her open, she'd bleed brown."

The look Delilah sent her said more than enough. She thought Harper was crazy. And she sort of was sometimes. It felt good, to say weird stuff. Out-of-character stuff.

Like being rude to Weston. She still couldn't believe she'd had it in her, but wow, she was proud. He deserved it. Though it hadn't seemed to bother him. She got the sense he found her angry comments amusing.

The jackass.

She shouldn't care. She'd moved on from that one moment—or so she told herself. She had a special someone in her life and had for a while now. Roger was everything she'd looked for in a man. Steady, reliable, loyal. With a good job and a good head on his shoulders, he was attractive and considerate and respected. They'd been together for just over a year and their relationship was solid.

So why did seeing West make her feel all tingly inside?

"Why were you so rude to West?" Delilah asked point-blank, as if reading her mind.

Harper chewed her lower lip, contemplating how to answer. The truth was too…truthful. What made it worse? Delilah used to go with West. Yeah, yeah, it was a long time ago when they'd been in high school, but still. They'd both burned bright together, running through town like they owned it and causing a bunch of trouble before they split.

Harper wasn't the type to poach on her friend's boyfriends, past or present—and especially future. Thinking lusty thoughts about West was normal. Thinking she could turn a single kissing session with West into a relationship was a joke. He belonged to no one. He never really had.

That was what made him so appealing. Weston Gallagher was…wild. Untamed. To her younger, much more romantic heart, he'd been the sort to send her swooning. The fact that she knew the word *swooning* was a testament to how many romance novels she had devoured over the years, amazing books she'd snatched from her grandma's hall closet. They'd filled her imagination with all sorts of unbelievably romantic things, and West had become the star in her overly imaginative fantasies.

She'd crushed on him since her early teens. And it hadn't helped spending all her free time at the Gallagher household. She saw West constantly. He'd teased her. Tricked her. Made her smile. Made her laugh. Made her sigh in pure, teenage misery when he dated an endless list of girls who were never, ever her. Eventually she got over it and moved on, forging her own way. Though in the back of her mind, that little spark of lust she felt for West never burned out…

And that one night, when for some unexplained reason he'd noticed her—*really* noticed her—and proceeded to drive her out of her mind with his delicious, wondrous mouth, she'd thought they actually had the potential to *be* something. He'd drugged her with his mouth. His touch. It was like they couldn't pry their lips from each other's for at least two hours. Maybe longer.

Her skin went hot just thinking about it. They'd been young and stupid, and he'd been a little drunk. She'd been neck deep in a massive crush for her best friend's brother, and what a freaking disaster that had turned out to be. When she realized he'd left town and never even bothered to tell her? She'd been so incredibly upset. He hadn't told anyone. Just…confessed to Lane and his parents that he was leaving the morning after the party, and then he was gone. Wren had been the one who told her he was gone. At first, Harper had been upset, wondering what she'd done to make him leave.

Then she got good and mad.

"We've never gotten along," she finally said, offering Delilah a kind smile. "I know you have a soft spot for him, but the two of us…I was always at his house when I was a kid, and he gave me endless grief. He and Holden terrorized Wren and me."

"But still. I've never seen you talk like that to anyone. Not even Bryan Atkins when he dumped you on prom night right in front of everyone," Delilah pointed out.

Harper barely held in the sigh that wanted to escape her. This was the problem with growing up in a small town and never leaving. Everyone knew her secrets. It hadn't mattered that Delilah was a year older than her. They'd hung in the same social circles because the circles were so damn small.

"Bryan Atkins was an asshole," Harper muttered as she started for the front of the store. Delilah fell into step beside her. "I haven't thought of him in years."

"I figured. No surprise considering you let him walk away from you so easily that night. I would've kneed my date in the balls if he had done something like that," Delilah said as she walked briskly by Harper's side. Harper would never shake her. Not that she really wanted to, but...

She didn't want to talk about Bryan Atkins, or anyone else for that matter. No, she wanted to savor the moment of seeing West for the first time in ages. She'd gotten a ~~good look at~~ him—and he at her—before he ran away from her like a coward. His sky blue eyes had studied her with a warmth and curiosity that intrigued her despite her long-held resentment toward him.

He was taller and broader than the last time they'd been in each other's presence. That white T-shirt he wore stretched over his muscles quite nicely. Too nicely. His jeans fit—very well.

Harper cleared her throat. She was sounding more and more like her grandma in her own head. More like she should think how great his ass looked in those jeans—because it did, it looked freaking amazing. But no. She went the staid, boring route, even in her thoughts. Did that mean she was turning into a prissy old woman?

God, she hoped not. She should ask Roger. He'd be honest with her. He was honest to a fault. They worked together—both literally and figuratively. She was the office manager of his accounting firm and they made a terrific pair. A solid team.

"Bryan wasn't worth my anger," Harper said with a gentle smile.

Gentle and *kind*, those were the two words her grandma used to describe her the most. Not a little spitfire or feisty or strong or even bitchy. Nope. Her claim to fame was being gentle and kind. Harper hated those two words with a burning passion. What would people think if she was aggressive and mean? Wouldn't that throw them for a loop? She'd always yearned to tear down those kind, gentle walls she'd built around herself over the years and just act…crazy. Out of her damn mind. Do whatever she wanted and damn the consequences.

But Harper had never done anything like that in her entire life. Roger would probably be horrified if she acted out that way. He wasn't one for making a big scene. He was as calm and gentle and kind as she was.

"And West is worth it? He's not so bad," Delilah said, waving a dismissive hand. "Harmless. I'm sure he gave you and Wren endless grief when you were kids, but I know he always liked you."

"He did?" Harper tried her best not to sound too shocked—or interested. Had he actually talked about her? To Delilah?

She'd figured she never registered on his radar growing up, beyond being his sister's best friend. He'd been too busy getting in trouble for various things—like bringing a flask of vodka to the homecoming dance, wrecking his car after an illegal street race when he was sixteen and practically failing out of school his junior year. He'd straightened up a little by the time he was a senior, but still. Everyone knew that Weston was trouble.

"Oh yeah. You know, we always remained friends, even after we broke up," Delilah said. "Our relationship had always been based more on friendship anyway."

Really? Harper wanted to ask, but she kept her mouth shut, which she knew was wise. If she asked too many questions she'd look suspicious. And Delilah was perceptive as all get out.

"That's…nice." Harper didn't know what else to say as they approached the registers and stood in line together. She glanced around the store, hoping she appeared nonchalant as she searched for West. Was he still here? Or had he already bailed out?

Ah, there he was. Two registers over, grabbing his receipt from the young female checker who gazed at him in blatant adoration. Harper couldn't see his face, but that was all right. West had plenty to ogle from behind too. Broad shoulders, a tapered back, and that perfect butt she'd never had the nerve to touch…

Ugh. Why was she checking him out? And worse…why was she thinking about touching his *butt*? She had a man. Roger was handsome. Maybe he wasn't as tall and built like West, but Roger had a very fit body. Though when was the last time she saw him naked? Not that they had sex with the lights on much. More like never at all. Roger always wanted to do it in the dark…

Harper frowned. Why were they always in the dark? Maybe she wanted to see him. Maybe she wanted to see herself. Ooh, maybe she wanted a mirror to watch them actually have sex. Though really, she could never imagine Roger and her staring at themselves in a mirror during sex. West though? Oh yeah, she could totally see him doing something like that. All the while whispering dirty things in her ear. Wicked, naughty things that would make her blush and moan and beg for more.

And she could *see* herself with him. Wrapped up in his strong arms, his hands on her, urging her to watch...

She shook herself, embarrassed by her own thoughts. How could she let herself get so caught up in a West fantasy? What in the world was wrong with her? Imagining herself in bed with him when she had a perfectly good boyfriend waiting for her at home. Though things had become rather stale between them lately. She adored Roger. Really she did. But he never made her feel even a fizzle of excitement like West did...

At that exact moment West glanced over his shoulder, their gazes meeting. Holding. She sucked in a breath, completely tuning Delilah out as she chattered away. All Harper could do was stare. She parted her lips, remembering what it felt like to have him surround her, his mouth on her neck, his hot breath tickling her throat as he made his secret confessions.

"I've had a thing for you for too damn long, Harper. Always wondered what it would be like if you were mine."

A shiver moved down her spine. Possessive. That's what West was. Had always been. The way he was looking at her this very moment felt as if he'd physically grabbed her and wasn't about to let her go.

She turned away from him first, smiling at Delilah and offering a murmured "oh no" luckily at the right time. When she chanced another glance in his direction…

West was gone.

Chapter Two

"SAW DELILAH TODAY at the new supermarket," West said as he flipped the burgers over on the grill before he shut the lid, turning to face his two brothers sitting on his back patio in his new outdoor chairs. Though the place had come mostly furnished, he had ended up going out and buying a few things to make the condo more his.

He failed to mention Harper on purpose. There was no need to bring her up. He shouldn't be thinking about her. How pretty she looked, how fiery her eyes had been when they landed on him...

Yeah. He shouldn't think about her at all.

"Cute as ever, right?" Holden grinned and took a sip from his beer. He was the youngest Gallagher and acted like it too. Their mother had overindulged him since he was a baby. Kid could get away with anything back then and most likely still could. He was forever the golden child. Always. Made West crazy.

"She looked good." West's voice remained neutral on purpose. He looked to his big brother, wondering what he might have to say about her. "Dee mentioned she's always talking to you, Lane."

Lane's expression didn't so much as flicker. "I see Delilah often, yeah." He nodded his confirmation, his tone of voice revealing nothing. Maybe West had imagined Delilah's reaction.

"Why's that?" Nah, West hadn't imagined anything. He remembered the way Delilah's cheeks went pink at the first mention of Lane. When they were dating back in high school, they used to make fun of his big brother and what a boring jerk he'd been. Now?

He had a sneaking suspicion that his ex-girlfriend was hot for his jerk of a brother.

Lane appeared completely put out at having to explain himself. "Work, bro. I patrol the shopping center where her dance studio's at." He took a swig from his beer and then nodded toward the barbecue grill. "How are those burgers coming? I'm starved."

Muttering under his breath, West lifted the lid on the grill and flipped the burgers once more. He'd wanted to have his brothers over at his new place tonight as a way to ease back into Gallagher family life. He hadn't been back to Wildwood for years. Not even for the holidays. Once he was gone, he was out, despite his mother's requests that he come home at least for Christmas. But he never had. His entire family probably thought he was a jerk, but at the time, he hadn't cared. He'd never planned on coming back either. The town was too small. Everyone knew who he was, knew all of his business. There was no such thing as keeping a secret in Wildwood. For once in his life he'd wanted to be anonymous.

The moment he could make his escape, he'd done it. Gladly. His mother had cried when he'd told her his promotion involved a transfer. She cried more because he'd told her about it at the last minute, right before he left. He couldn't help but think that was a total jackass move. But then his father had told him he'd be back in a knowing tone. That one remark had stung. Had driven West to prove that he would never, ever come back.

Someone should've told him a long time ago, never say never.

So here he was, back in his hometown, all because of another transfer. When he went to the interview for the permanent engineer position in the ranger unit he'd started in, he'd known what he was doing. He knew what it looked like when they asked him about returning to Wildwood and the outlying area. Everyone probably figured he was purposely trying to come back home.

That wasn't West's plan though. This was a pit stop, nothing more. He'd work at the Wildwood Lake station for a few years before transferring out at his first chance to be promoted to captain. He was all about climbing the promotional ladder as fast as he could. He loved what he did. He was good at his job too. But the better the position, the more people would respect him—like his father. If that meant coming home for a few years, then so be it.

If he could prove to everyone that he wasn't the fuckup they all thought he was, even better. He'd rather leave in a blaze of glory, unlike last time when he'd fled Wildwood like the unwanted son.

"When's your first shift start?" Lane asked him.

West glanced at him over his shoulder. "Two days." Though he was going in tomorrow to meet everyone, get his bearings.

"Hey, I go back to work in two days," Holden added, amusement filling his voice. "Too bad we're not at the same station."

Thank Christ they weren't at the same station. West didn't think he could handle it. Bossing around his little brother didn't sound like fun. Holden had never done well with authority, and that was putting it mildly.

Like West had any room to judge. He'd fought against authority—namely their father—since he was a little kid.

"Your condo is nice," Lane said, changing the subject when West still hadn't acknowledged Holden's comment. "I assume you're renting it?"

"Yeah, didn't want to bother buying because I don't know how long I'm going to stay here," West explained.

"You don't want to stay?" Holden sounded incredulous. And why wouldn't he? He had all the comforts of home here in Wildwood. Mom and Dad doted on him. His girlfriend, Kirsten, whom he'd been dating since they were in high school, was loyal and sweet. Everyone assumed Holden would marry her eventually. They were what everyone called the perfect couple.

That sounded like a total trap to West. Oh, Kirsten was a nice girl and all, but marriage? Holden was only twenty-three, just a baby in West's eyes.

"You gonna give us a tour after dinner?" Lane asked, his eyebrows raised.

"Absolutely." West could admit that he wanted to show off his place. The older three-bedroom, one-and-a-half-bath condominium was close to the lake, perfect rental property for tourists. He'd struck a deal with the owner, thankful for once that he was from Wildwood and still knew how to pull a few strings.

After all, the owner was none other than Rebecca Hill—Harper's grandmother.

"Saw Harper Hill at the supermarket, too," West said as he turned off the burners on the barbecue. He scooped the burgers off the grill with his new spatula and set them on a paper plate, then brought them over to the table where they were going to eat. "She's looking...good too."

That sounded awkward as hell and he braced himself, waiting for them to say something, anything to give him endless shit. He shouldn't have mentioned her, but he was digging. Looking for any bit of information he could get on Harper.

But they didn't say a word. Lane looked at West's pitiful offerings of mustard and ketchup before lifting his gaze. "You went to the fancy supermarket and this is all you got for our burgers?"

"And some chips." West waved an unopened bag of potato chips at Lane.

"You need some serious domestication," Holden declared as he put together his hamburger and took a big bite out of it. "You live too much like a bachelor," he said, his mouth full.

"Aren't we all bachelors?" West asked. Lane lived alone. Supposedly so did Holden though everyone knew Kirsten spent most of her time at his apartment in town.

"Well, I've got Kirsten, and Lane is like an old man, so I would say we've got this eating properly thing down," Holden teased. "You, on the other hand, probably only have a twelve-pack and those condiments filling your fridge."

West grimaced but said nothing. Whatever. So Holden was right, so what? He didn't need to be domesticated, to have some woman always telling him what to do. He liked living on his own, not needing anyone. He was perfectly content. If he wanted female company, he went out and found it. It wasn't that hard.

They ate in silence, but West wasn't uncomfortable. This was normal for them growing up. Their parents had civilized conversation—if Dad was even home. He'd worked long hours, and when he was off, he rarely made an appearance, even during mealtime, especially when he and Lane were teenagers. The boys had shoveled food in their faces while Wren did all the gabbing. She was good at it. As they got older, she usually had a friend accompanying her at the dinner table too, resulting in endless, loud female chatter.

Usually that friend was Harper.

Since arriving in Wildwood, his mind seemed to keep circling back to her, and he wondered at that. Wondered too, at the way he'd caught her staring at him just before he left the store earlier today. The look in her eyes had been downright...hungry, which had surprised him. And he'd immediately felt an answering hunger deep inside. One borne of curiosity and familiarity, one he wanted to explore further, even though he knew it was a huge mistake.

He blamed it on the kiss they'd shared. Well, kisses. Why else would he be so hung up on a girl he'd known most of his life? Fine, that one summer when he'd gone for it, when he'd been a little drunk and full of liquid courage and basically attacked her—in a good way, not a creeper way—it had been hot as hell. *She* was hot as hell. So damn responsive and soft in all the right places, with those warm, damp lips and sweet sighs and the way she said his name...

Frowning, West stood and gathered up everyone's empty plates and crumpled napkins without asking, taking it all into the kitchen and dumping it in the trash. Lane followed him inside, Holden on his heels, the both of them going for the fridge so they could each grab another beer.

"Give us the tour," Lane practically commanded after he shut the refrigerator door, twisting the cap off the beer he held and tossing it in the garbage can.

West gritted his teeth and did exactly that, hustling them through his new place. The condo was small so the tour lasted approximately thirty seconds, and that worked for him. He suddenly wanted his brothers out of there. Fast.

He wanted to be alone.

"Harper used to live here," Holden said conversationally as he glanced around the master bedroom, swigging from his beer bottle.

West frowned and turned to look at his brother. "She did?" Well, that didn't really surprise him considering her grandmother owned the place. But he didn't like that Holden knew this, and happened to mention that particular fact while they were in the bedroom, which West could only assume used to be Harper's old bedroom.

West's gaze slid to the bed. Had she slept there? Most likely. And why did that give him a weird, hot twist in his stomach?

"Yeah," Holden said with a nod. "Before she moved in with her boyfriend."

West was seriously glad he hadn't been drinking something when Holden made that statement. He probably would've spit out his beer. Harper had a live-in boyfriend? For real?

"Who's her boyfriend?" He was surprised his voice sounded so neutral, so normal. Deep inside that hot twist turned into a full-on painful cramp.

"Roger Bowman," Lane said, stopping to stand in the doorway. West turned to look at him, wanting to hear more yet not wanting any details about Harper's love life with someone else. He didn't like thinking of her with any other guy.

Meaning he was a selfish asshole.

"He moved here right after you left," Lane explained. "Runs his own accounting firm."

An accountant. Of course Harper had found herself a stable, quiet nerd—er, numbers—man. He couldn't help but wonder if good ol' Roger Bowman wore a pocket protector. Glasses maybe? Short-sleeved button-up shirts with a tie that looked like it was strangling him?

Okay, now he was just being a judgmental asshole.

"That's great," West said with a nod, hating the catch in his throat. "Harper deserves nothing but happiness."

And he meant every last word.

THE MOMENT HARPER pulled into the driveway of the small cottage she shared with Roger she knew something wasn't right.

She shifted into park and turned off the engine of her Corolla, staring at the house as she listened to the engine tick in the otherwise quiet. It was past eight, and even though the sky was staying lighter later and later as the official start of summer drew closer, there was usually at least one lamp blazing from within the house.

But every window was eerily dark, despite Roger's car parked in the driveway right next to hers. They didn't use the garage because it was too full of Roger's crap, or um, stuff. He was a collector of every video game action figure known to man, from what Harper could see. She understood collections. Her mother and grandmother had been obsessed with Beanie Babies years ago when she was a kid, and they'd done everything humanly possible to grow their collection, always dragging Harper along with them.

Harper prided herself on being a very understanding person, even though that might've meant she was also a very boring person. But damn it, people didn't understand enough most of the time—all anyone usually wanted was to be heard. Acknowledged. She was a good listener. A soother, if there was such a thing. And that was what drew her to Roger in the first place. He was a sensitive soul. Sweet and caring and quiet. Smart. So smart he made her feel dumb sometimes, though he never meant to.

Frowning, she grabbed her shopping bag from her earlier excursion at the supermarket and exited the car, heading toward the front door. Her steps were brisk, her sandals slapping across the sidewalk as she hurried to get into the warm house. It might have been close to summer, but the air still turned cold quick, considering Wildwood's high elevation. She wrapped her fingers around the cool metal door handle, turning it, fully expecting it to be unlocked, but it wasn't.

Huh.

She pulled her keys out of her purse and unlocked the door, bursting in with a soft hello that seemed to echo throughout the tiny house. She set her purse on the table right beside the front door and went into the dark kitchen, putting the few items she'd picked up at the supermarket away in the pantry.

Still no sign of Roger.

Double huh.

Slowly she walked through the house, down the hall toward their bedroom. The door was shut. An uneasy feeling slid down her spine, settling low in her stomach, making it churn. With shaking fingers she reached out, grabbed hold of the doorknob and turned it.

The door creaked open and she peeked her head around it, wincing in preparation for what would most likely be some sort of devastating, horrible image she'd never be able to scrub from her brain no matter how hard she tried. Roger writhing around on their bed with an unknown woman. Or perhaps the woman would be straddling Roger, naked and riding him for all he's worth.

Harper frowned. Roger had never been a big fan of her on top. They always did it missionary style. Lately they hadn't been doing it much at all…

Her gaze landed on the bed, her shoulders stiff, breath lodged in her throat, fully prepared for what she might see. But there was no woman writhing around with Roger on their bed, locked in a passionate embrace. And there certainly wasn't a woman riding her boyfriend for all he was worth. Instead, it was only Roger, lying on his side in the middle of the queen-size bed, practically curled into a ball, sleeping soundly.

She closed the door just as softly as she'd opened it, tiptoeing back out into the living room, where she collapsed on the couch with a barely contained sigh of…relief? That's what she should be feeling.

So the disappointment Harper experienced at finding him alone wasn't a good thing. But that was exactly what she felt: complete and utter disappointment. What the hell was wrong with her? Did she really want Roger to cheat on her?

No. Though that would've at least stirred up some excitement in her life, right?

Leaning back against the soft, chocolate-brown microsuede couch, she closed her eyes. She was being ridiculous. So she and Roger had been going through a rough patch. Make that more of a…boring patch. Yes, their relationship had turned boring quickly. Like the moment they moved in together. At first, she'd loved it. Loved making Roger dinner and watching him work out in the tiny backyard on the weekends, completing all of those tasks she put on his honey-do list. Loved sharing a bed with him every night, enjoyed the sweet, thoughtful sex they experienced.

Harper made a face, keeping her eyes closed. Who had sweet, thoughtful sex? God, that sounded so pathetically boring. And that was the problem. Everything about her and Roger had turned…

Boring. With a capital, giant, bold-ass B.

"Hey."

Opening her eyes, she found Roger standing in front of her, a little rumpled, a lot confused. His glasses were perched crookedly on his nose, and she wanted to reach out and straighten them. Smooth out his hair, brush her hands down the front of his wrinkled shirt. Roger wasn't one to appear rumpled. He had an image to uphold, even when he was home with just her.

She did none of those things though. Instead she offered him a hey in return.

"I didn't know you were home," Roger said as he settled on the couch beside her, leaving a few inches between them. Within reaching distance though, and that was a good thing. It *had* to be a good thing. Maybe they weren't a passionate, overcome-with-need-for-each-other couple, but comfortable was good. Comfortable was safe.

And Harper liked feeling safe.

"I didn't want to disturb you," Harper said, settling her hand in the empty space between them, picking at a non-existent loose thread. She wanted to see if Roger would reach for her hand and entwine their fingers. It wasn't fair, what she was doing. Testing him. She couldn't help it though. Besides, she was testing herself just as much.

"I was so tired when I got home from work I just collapsed on the bed and crashed." He sent her a rueful smile. "And it's not even tax season anymore."

Her smile was strained while panic ate at her insides. Oh, God, she couldn't do this. Not with Roger. She'd been fooling herself thinking that he was the one. He so wasn't. She worked for him, they spent all of their time together, yet she'd never felt so disconnected from someone in her entire life. They'd lived together for the last six months, and it just…it wasn't working. They were good friends, but that was it.

Did he realize it? Did he see that they weren't what anyone would call a passionate, madly in love couple? She'd been feeling that way for a while, keeping her worry to herself, but after what had happened today her fears were confirmed.

If she was really happy with Roger, then she wouldn't have had such a strong reaction to Weston.

The moment she'd set eyes on West, her entire body had broken out in goose bumps. When their gazes first met, she'd been instantly transported back to that singular hot night they'd shared. The night he'd approached her with a drunken, crooked smile and asked if she'd take a walk with him. She'd said yes like an eager puppy, and he'd seemed just as eager, taking her hand and dragging her along with him.

They'd found a secluded alcove near the lake. He'd wrapped her up in his arms when she complained that she was cold and proceeded to warm her up with his lips and hands for hours. It had been the most passionate night of her life, hands down. A make-out session, one that West had most likely *forgotten*, was the most passionate encounter she'd ever experienced.

How sad was that?

But she wanted that. Craved it. Passion. Longing. Heat. Lots and lots of heat. Glancing over at Roger now, she felt no heat. Well, there was that pleasant warmth lingering within her, but it felt like friendship. Fondness. None of that passionate, overwhelming burn that threatened to consume her.

That's what she wanted, what she needed. Yet what she and Roger shared didn't even come close to passion.

Taking a deep breath, she reached out and patted Roger's hand, offering him a sad smile. "Roger, I think we need to talk."

Chapter Three

"AND SO WE both agreed, I'm moving out." Harper shrugged and reached for her coffee, taking a sip. "I spent the night at Grandma's. I'll be staying there through the weekend and then I'll go in Monday when Roger's at work and get all my stuff moved out." Where she was going to go, she wasn't sure, but she'd figure it out.

She had to.

Her best friend, Wren Gallagher, gaped at her, mouth dropping open, her eyes wide with what Harper knew was shock. Eyes that were as blue as her brother's, if Harper was being truthful. Why hadn't she ever really noticed it before? West and Wren shared the same eyes, as well as the same initials.

"Wait a minute." Wren shook her head. "*You* broke up with Roger?"

Harper nodded, remaining quiet.

"But why?" Wren asked incredulously.

She knew her best friend would ask that question. She would've done the same if the tables were turned. The problem?

Harper really didn't have an answer. Not a good one, at least. What could she say? That she wanted burning passion—which probably wasn't real, just something out of a romance novel, but she wanted to try for it anyway? Yeah, Wren would look at her like she was crazy.

Maybe she was. It didn't really matter. She couldn't string Roger along any further. He was a good guy looking for a woman to spend the rest of his life with. He deserved to be with a woman who really wanted him and loved him for who he was. Not a woman who'd settled because she thought that's what she should do.

"He deserved better," Harper finally said, her voice soft. She didn't want too many people to overhear her. Word of their relationship's demise would be out by the end of the day anyway. Living in a small town, anything that happened was duly reported and spread around like crazy. The story of Harper and Roger splitting would be a big one. Everyone had assumed they'd eventually get married, including, at one point, Harper.

Wren blinked at her. "*He* deserved better?" She leaned across the table, her voice lowering to a soft whisper. "What about you? You deserve better too, you know. I always thought…" Her voice drifted and she clamped her lips shut.

"What?" Harper prodded. "Just spit it out. You know you want to."

"Roger is sweet as pie, but he's so *boring*." Wren practically spit the last word out. "Seriously, Harper. This might be the best thing you could've ever done for yourself. Now you're *free*."

She wanted to believe what Wren said was true. That this was a good move. A smart move. But what if it wasn't? She'd never really felt trapped with Roger. What they shared had been nice. Pleasant. Maybe that was all she could ever hope for. What if she never found a man as good as Roger? What then?

Panic had hit her hard last night in her grandmother's too small and rather lumpy guest bed. What was she supposed to do now? Where could she go? She refused to move back home. Her parents—specifically her mother—loved to run her life and the minute she stepped back into her childhood home, it would feel like she was giving her mother the reins to take over once more. Or worse, that she'd somehow failed at being an adult and had to move back home at the age of twenty-six.

No thank you.

"You really think this was a good move for me?" Harper asked tentatively. She glanced around the coffee shop, thankful she saw no one she knew. It was mostly filled with tourists and she was glad.

Like, really glad. She didn't think she was ready to face all the questions, the sympathetic looks, the reassurances that everything would be okay. And yeah, she knew everything would eventually be okay.

Well. She hoped so.

"Of course." Wren smiled. "And now we're both single together! This is a rare occurrence. We should go out tonight and celebrate."

"Celebrate?" Harper shook her head. "Shouldn't I be in mourning or something? Roger and I were together for over a year. We *lived* together, Wren. And you want me to go out with you tonight so we can party and get drunk?" That wouldn't look good, would it? Out on a Saturday night with her best friend and without a care in the world? While Roger stayed at home and cried over the loss of his fickle girlfriend?

Okay, he probably wouldn't be crying. He'd actually taken the news like a champ and said that he'd felt the same way, which came as a surprise to her. He knew she'd felt restless lately and he was worried that he wouldn't be enough for her. That had made her feel bad.

Until he said that she wasn't enough for him either.

Wren waved a hand. "You worry too much over what people think about you. You always have."

"And you don't worry enough." This was why they made such a good team. They balanced each other out.

"Fine, let's go out tonight and you can cry into your glass of white wine while you slowly get drunk. Same diff." Wren smiled, looking like she'd just solved world peace. "You need to let loose, Harper. Roger kept you all stifled up in that little house of his and you never wanted to go out anymore. I've finally got you back." Wren made a face. "I sound incredibly selfish, don't I?"

"Sort of." Harper reached out and grabbed her hand, clasping it between both of hers. "But I don't mind. You're right. I was so busy trying to make sure what Roger and I had was working that I probably neglected our friendship." She'd neglected everything, including her own needs. And she did have needs, damn it. "I'm sorry."

"You don't need to apologize, it's okay. Really. I understand. Men make us do crazy things." Wren smiled and withdrew her hand from Harper's. "Speaking of men, I know some of my brothers are going out tonight. We should go with them."

Just like that, nerves jumped in Harper's stomach. "Which brothers?" *Please say Holden and Lane. Please, please say Holden and Lane.*

"Holden and West." Wren wrinkled her nose. "That jerk invited them over for dinner last night but didn't include me. Can you believe it?"

"Which jerk?" Harper knew which one. She just...what? Wanted to hear his name said out loud again? Wanted to talk about him in the sneakiest way possible?

She was pitiful. If Wren knew she was hot for West she'd probably...

Harper didn't know what Wren would do. She'd tried her hardest to keep her brothers away from her friends, which had been impossible. Boys surrounded Wren in her house. When they were younger, all of Wren's friends had wanted to go over there after school and on the weekends for a chance to hang out with the Gallagher boys, including Harper. Though she never admitted it. Wren really was her friend.

She just happened to have a minor crush on her best friend's big brother.

"West. He's such an ass. Why wouldn't he invite me? Is it because I don't have a penis?" Wren's head jerked toward the entrance, her eyes narrowing. "Uh-oh, look who just walked in."

Harper ducked her head, glancing as slyly as she could toward the door, fully expecting to see West striding inside. But it wasn't him.

"What's the big deal? It's just Tate." Harper turned to face Wren once more, only to find her friend wasn't paying her any mind. She was too busy staring at the handsome firefighter as he made his way to the counter to place his order.

"He acts like he's God's gift to women," Wren all but sneered.

Well, Tate Warren was extremely handsome. And he knew it too, with that perfect smile he was always flashing at innocent women and the way he drew attention whenever he was in his uniform, considering he filled it out oh-so-finely. Harper was of the quiet assumption that Tate wore it more often than was necessary just so he could make women drool.

And they were drooling right now. Well, except for Harper. She was too busy saving her drool for a certain someone who was related to her best friend, who she'd bet a million bucks also filled out his uniform oh-so-finely.

Wren? She was glaring at Tate like she wanted to rip his head off. Or his clothes.

Huh.

"What's your deal?" Harper asked, leaning across the table so Tate wouldn't overhear them. "You look like you want to gouge his eyes out."

"That wouldn't be a bad idea." Wren grimaced. "He's a jerk."

"He's been nothing but nice to me," Harper defended. "I like him."

"Right, because you were protected in your cozy little relationship. Wait until Tate finds out you're single. He'll try and make a move on you, I'm sure," Wren said bitterly.

"Wait a minute." Harper frowned. "Did he try to do that to you?"

Wren blinked. "Do what?"

"Make a move on you?" And if so, why hadn't Wren gone for it? Tate was gorgeous. And nice. And hot. Close in age. Oh and single, a rarity in Wildwood.

"Wren Gallagher."

They both glanced up to find Tate standing right next to their table, smiling down at them, his hands on his hips. Harper leaned back in her chair, smiling at him in return, but all Wren managed was a glower.

Yikes.

"Harper." Tate nodded, his green eyes twinkling. Oh, he was pretty. Why hadn't she ever noticed it before? Had she been so focused on making it work with Roger that she hadn't noticed the other good-looking men in her life? "Good morning."

Harper parted her lips, ready to wish him a good morning as well when her best friend interrupted her.

"Why are you in your uniform?" Wren asked, rolling her eyes. "Trying to turn on the ladies?"

"Considering you're the only one I want to turn on and yet you're immune to my charms, Gallagher, that would be a no." He turned his attention to Harper. "I just got off work. Thought I'd grab a coffee and a doughnut, then go crash for a few hours."

"Tough shift?" Harper asked politely. She'd always liked Tate. He'd come to Wildwood just over a year ago and fit right in like he was homegrown. He was nice, if a little egotistical sometimes, cocky but never rudely arrogant. And he had reason to be. Women seriously fell at his feet. She saw it happen once out at the lake last summer while he'd been out on a call. The woman had literally fainted on top of his booted feet.

He came by his reputation rather naturally.

"Brutal. But what else is new? We're out there fighting fires and saving lives." He returned his gaze to Wren, letting it linger. "I hear your brother starts his first shift at my station tomorrow."

Wren nodded. "He sure does." She said the words like she was reluctant to even speak to him.

"Well. Can't wait to meet him. If he's anything like Holden I'm sure we'll get along fine." The barista called Tate's name, and he winked at them before he started to walk away. "See you later, ladies."

"Something in your eye, Tate?" Wren called after him but he ignored her, too busy chatting up the cute barista who was batting her eyelashes at him.

"What was that about?" Harper asked as soon as Tate left the coffee shop.

Wren shrugged. "He's annoying."

Uh-huh. Just like Harper found West so annoying. "What did he ever do to you?"

"I don't know. Breathe?" Wren rolled her eyes and laughed. "I'm ridiculous, I know it. But there's something about him that bothers me. He's so...sure of himself."

Most women would find that an attractive quality.

"His attitude borders on arrogant. He always smirks at me, like he knows my deepest darkest secrets no matter how much I try to hide from him."

"Are you trying to hide secrets from Tate?" Harper asked.

"Of course not," Wren said quickly. "I've grown up around firefighters my entire life. They're nothing special, even Tate."

Hmm. There was more here than met the eye.

And Harper was dying to know exactly what it was.

THE MOMENT THEY entered the bar, West saw her. Sitting with his sister, her auburn head bent toward Wren's, her perfect mouth stretched wide in a smile as she listened to whatever his sister had to say.

Lord knew Wren always had something to say. The woman never stopped talking.

Holden and Kirsten had wanted to take him out for a celebratory drink before he started his shift at the Wildwood station tomorrow. Considering he had to be there bright and early at seven in the morning, he had zero plans to get wasted. He wanted to make a good impression on not only his fire captain, but also the firefighters who would be under his supervision.

His little brother and Kirsten, on the other hand, had already downed a six-pack between them at home by the time West had stopped by to pick them up fifteen minutes ago. They were well on their way to Drunkville, and Holden had to be at work tomorrow morning just like West did. But Holden was younger. He'd bounce back easier.

Hopefully.

"Ah, good, Wren's here!" Kirsten shouted, making West grimace. "And look, Harper's here too."

His body went on high alert at hearing her name, and got even worse when he got a better look at her. She was wearing some flirty flower print dress with little sleeves that showed off her slender arms, a scooped neckline that dipped low though not scandalously low. Her hair was up in a ponytail, showing off her neck. A pretty neck he was immediately tempted to kiss again. She sat on the barstool with her legs crossed, the very tops of her thighs exposed, along with the rest of her legs, simple black sandals on her feet. All that skin was bared, on display. Not in a vulgar way. No one could ever call Harper Hill vulgar. But considering he'd had his lips on her skin before, knew her taste, knew the way she'd suck in a breath when his lips touched a particular spot, well...

Seeing all that beautiful, smooth skin, he was tempted to put his mouth all over her, all over again.

She has a boyfriend, asshole. You need to rein it in.

Right. He needed to remember that.

Kirsten was running toward the girls while Holden and West trailed after her. The bar was crowded—it was mostly locals at the Forks Bar on a Saturday night and it was still early in the season. West heard a few people call his name and he smiled and nodded, not in the mood to try to make small talk or worse, catch up after he'd been gone for so many years. He suddenly had only one goal tonight:

Get close to Harper.

Catch a whiff of her mysterious scent. Maybe touch her—innocently of course. She was a taken woman. Hell, she lived with the guy. And why that felt like such a kick in the gut, West wasn't sure. He didn't want to analyze it too closely either.

"I'm mad at you," Wren said the moment he approached.

West frowned. "Why? What'd I do?"

"You didn't invite me to your Gallagher family dinner last night. Though I guess you wouldn't considering it was men only." She crossed her arms in front of her chest, clearly bent out of shape.

"It's not like I purposely excluded you," West defended, hoping like hell Harper wouldn't think less of him for not inviting his sister to last night's lame-ass dinner. He figured Wren would've turned him down anyway. Why would she want to hang out with her three annoying brothers? Of course, she'd always tried to tag along when they were younger…

"Whatever. I'm sure it sucked anyway. Not like I missed anything." Wren waved a hand, clearly already over it. Plus, the bartender had just set two shot glasses in front of the girls. Wren grinned madly at Harper as she handed one of the glasses to her. "Bottoms up!"

Harper hadn't even looked in his direction yet and he was surprisingly butt hurt. He watched as she grabbed the glass and clinked it to the edge of Wren's before tossing her head back and drinking that shot down in one smooth swallow. She made a sexy little satisfied noise as she slammed her now empty glass on the counter, wiping her mouth with the back of her hand and beaming at his sister.

Ah shit. Was that his dick twitching to life? He had no idea watching Harper *drink* would be so damn arousing. He needed to get himself in check and stat. She was a taken woman. He had no business lusting after her. She belonged to someone else.

The thought alone made his mouth dry as sand.

"I need a drink," he muttered to no one in particular.

"Want me to order you something?" Harper asked sweetly.

West did a double take, shock coursing through him. Did she just offer to do something nice for him? Yesterday when they talked she'd both insulted and snubbed him all in a matter of seconds. "Uh, sure. A beer?"

"Pale ale?" She lifted her brows.

His skin went warm. She remembered his favorite beer. Way to get to a man's heart and quick. "Yeah. That would be great. Thanks."

"Not a problem." She turned toward the bartender, waving her hand until she got his attention. He made his way over to where she and Wren sat and the both of them gave the guy an earful, orders from everyone.

But Harper asked for only West's order. Why that little detail made him feel special, he wasn't sure. He wasn't going to dwell on it. He couldn't. Nothing could happen between them. Not ever.

He had the urge to get a beer in hand even more now.

"We're celebrating," Wren told him when the bartender walked away.

He raised a brow. "What are you celebrating?"

"Wren." Harper's tone was a warning, and Wren pressed her lips together, looking like she might burst. "Don't say it."

Now he was curious. Though what if they were celebrating Harper's engagement to the dude she lived with? Hey, it could happen. Living with someone was quite the commitment. One he couldn't imagine wanting to embark on. He wasn't even ready for a relationship.

He didn't think he'd ever be ready.

Wren's lips parted and she sucked in air before she blurted, "Harper's a free woman."

West frowned, his gaze sliding to Harper's. "Free?"

Harper glared at his sister before she offered him a weak smile. "Um, my boyfriend and I…"

"She dumped him," Wren interrupted. "And about damn time too. He was *so boring.*"

Harper said nothing. Neither could West. His brain was too busy reworking what Wren had just told him. Harper was single. This was good news.

Excellent news.

"You promised you wouldn't bash him," Harper said quietly.

"I'm sorry. You know I get mouthy when I drink." Lamest excuse ever. Wren was always mouthy. "West, you're lucky you didn't witness those two together. They made a horrible couple."

He could see the hurt etched all over Harper's face, but she wasn't saying anything. "Wren, lay off."

"Please." Wren waved a hand. "Harper knows the truth. I mean, come on. They worked together, which was the first mistake. How exciting could an accountant be?"

West raised his brows. "Aren't *you* an accountant?" Would Harper continue working with her now ex-boyfriend? That would be…weird.

"Bookkeeper." Wren waved her hand around again, nearly slapping West's cheek. He dodged out of her way.

"Same diff," Harper muttered under her breath.

"You two aren't going to start fighting are you?" West asked warily. They used to when they were kids, over stupid girl stuff that drove him up the damn wall.

"Did someone say the word *catfight*?" A male voice asked from behind him. West turned to find a guy around his age smiling widely, his gaze only for Wren, who glared at him in return. "I'd pay money to see you tumble around with your bestie, Gallagher, especially if the clothes start flying off." He started to laugh.

West frowned. Who was this dude? And why was he calling Wren by her last name? Clearly it bugged the shit out of her.

"Shut the hell up," Wren muttered, turning her charm onto the bartender, who approached with all the drinks. "Ooh, yay. I'm thirsty."

Harper grabbed West's beer from the counter and handed it to him, her fingers brushing against his when he took the bottle. Electricity sparked between them and he wondered at that. Remembered how it had been between them before. So hot, they'd nearly set each other on fire.

He wondered if that would happen again, was tempted to make a move on her if only to see if they could still create that heat.

But he couldn't. She just broke up with her live-in boyfriend. That was serious. She was probably nursing a broken heart. Was it wrong that he found her timing impeccable? Probably. Harper had *serious girlfriend* written all over her and he had *hey, let's get drunk and screw around for one night* written all over him.

Didn't mean he couldn't flirt with her for just a little bit tonight though. Test the waters, so to speak. "Thank you," he murmured, his voice low. Just for her. "Did I tell you that you look pretty tonight?"

Her cheeks turned the faintest pink. "Stop."

"I'm serious." He tipped the bottle to his lips and drank, the icy-cold beer sliding down his throat. She watched him the entire time, her gaze never leaving him, and he wondered at that too. "You were sort of rude to me at the supermarket yesterday," he said after he swallowed, setting his beer on the counter right next to her.

She made a little face. "I was having a bad day."

"And seeing me made it worse?" He was practically holding his breath waiting for her answer, which was crazy. "Never mind, don't answer that."

"Oh, no you don't. I want to answer your question." She touched him, her fingers pressing into his forearm, and he went completely still. "Seeing you didn't make my day worse. But it did bring up some…old memories."

"Good or bad ones?" He sounded nervous. Hell, he *was* nervous. There was something about Harper that set him on edge.

Harper parted her perfect pink lips, ready to say something just as Wren butted in.

"Weston, I forgot to introduce you to Tate Warren. He works at your station."

He turned to find the guy who called his sister by her last name smiling at him, holding his hand out. "Good to meet you, man," Tate said.

West shook his hand, getting the distinct feeling he was being sized up. Fine with him, considering he was sizing up Tate too. What the hell kind of name was Tate? Though he had no room to talk. His entire family had slightly unusual names.

"Nice meeting you too," West said. "What's your position? You a firefighter?" The guy couldn't be much older than him, maybe was even younger.

Tate grinned. "I'm your captain."

How could he not remember Warren's name? Oh yeah, he'd been interviewed by a panel of battalion chiefs, all of whom worked at the ranger unit's headquarters. So he'd never had a chance to actually meet his new captains.

"And we're ready to have you at the station," Tate continued. "Nothing better than knowing a Gallagher is coming to work with us. Your father is a freaking legend around these parts."

It took everything within him not to grimace. Or worse, tell his new captain to fuck off. He hated hearing anyone talk about his so-called legendary father.

The man merely did his job. He wasn't a legend. Yeah, he knew Holden ate that crap up with a giant gold spoon, but not West. He never had. The constant comparisons to his father were the main reason he got out of Wildwood.

Now he worried it might've been a major mistake to come back.

"Glad you think so highly of him," West said, his voice tight. He saw the questioning look in Tate's eyes and mentally told himself to relax. "Looking forward to working with you and everyone else this season."

"It's going to be crazy, I can practically guarantee it." Tate grinned again. "But we're ready. I'm figuring you are, too?"

The assured smile West offered him felt natural, as did the words that slipped past his lips.

"I was born ready."

Chapter Four

"SO YOU BROKE up with him." Rebecca Hill smiled at Harper, reaching out to pat her hand. "It was probably for the best. I never really thought the two of you suited."

Her grandmother slung the insult with a sweet smile so Harper really couldn't be offended. Her grandma hadn't approved of her relationship with Roger from the beginning, and Harper could never figure out why. Throughout her life she'd valued her grandma's opinion so much, but for once, she'd gone against her advice. Moving in with him had thrown practically the entire Hill family into a tizzy.

But Harper had thought they were going to get married and she'd gone for it anyway. Despite the disapproval. Despite her friends asking if being with Roger was what she really wanted. She'd ignored them all, firmly believing she knew best.

What made it worse? She'd have to quit her job. Working for Roger…she couldn't do it. Being essentially his secretary for the last two years? Why had she let herself become trapped in such a menial job? All for a man?

She almost wanted to slap herself.

"You were right," Harper admitted, swallowing past the bitter lump in her throat. "I should've listened to you."

"There, there." Her grandma patted her again before wrapping her hands around the large coffee mug sitting in front of her. "We all need to break free and try something on our own. Most of the time that involves not listening to what well-meaning people tell us. Unwanted and unasked-for advice is the worst, isn't it?"

The absolute worst. She'd already dealt with the lecture from her mom and had been thankful her father hadn't had much to say about it. She just wanted to move on and not focus on any of that anymore. What was done was done.

"When was your break-free moment?" Harper asked. If she said marrying Harper's grandpa, she'd want to bang her own head against a wall. Her grandparents had the sweetest relationship in the world. Everyone aspired to be them, including Harper. She'd been incredibly close to her grandpa, spending most of her time with him when she was little, up until he died unexpectedly when she was fifteen. She'd been devastated. The entire Hill family had been in a state of shock over the sudden loss. Her grandmother had mourned properly then soldiered on, and even eventually opened her own business.

And they were sitting in the same business at this very moment.

"After your grandfather died, there were all sorts of people offering up every little bit of advice you could imagine. Most of my friends, my family, and especially your father." Her eldest son. "They all wanted to tell me what to do next, how I should live my life, but I was still young! Despite being a grandma and settled, perfectly content in the life we'd created together, I knew I still had a lot of years in me. I wasn't going to die along with my husband."

Harper nodded, fighting the sadness that always threatened when they talked about her grandpa. She wished he were still here. He'd give her good advice about Roger. He'd give her good advice about anything and everything.

"Your grandpa died so quickly, it was shocking. And losing him like that immediately filled me with this sense of purpose I'd never felt before. I knew I had to stop worrying over what other people thought about me and do exactly what I wanted." Grandma glanced around the room, her eyes sparkling with amusement. "So I opened this place."

The Bigfoot Diner. It was the most kitschy, ridiculous restaurant in all of Wildwood, if not the entire county. An ode to her grandfather, who had loved anything and everything having to do with Bigfoot. He'd always said he wanted to open a restaurant that everyone would call the BFD. He'd talked about it for years, scoping out available restaurants when they were for sale, contemplating exactly how he would open one and what he would do. He'd even created a menu, giving the items creative Bigfoot-related names.

No one had taken him seriously. Except his wife.

No one thought it was a joke now. Everyone loved the Bigfoot Diner. It had the best hamburgers in town. All of the food was good. The restaurant's Yelp rating was a solid 4.6 and it had over one thousand reviews. Her grandma had taken her late husband's dream and turned it into a reality—and a total success.

"Your break-free moment was a positive one," Harper pointed out.

"I had many, many others that weren't so positive." Her grandma smiled. "You have to remember I've been around a lot longer than you, dear. You're still young. You still have many break-free moments to look forward to. Some of them will be mistakes, but don't let them get you down. That's just a part of life."

Harper took a deep breath and let it out slowly. She hoped her grandma was right. Breaking up with Roger so quickly hadn't allowed her much time to consider the other things that came with ending their relationship. Like…finding a new place to live. Finding a new job. She'd never describe herself as spontaneous, but this was by far the most spontaneous thing she'd ever done. "Do you mind if I stay with you for a while longer? Until I figure out what I'm going to do next?" she asked.

Her grandma gave her a look, one that said she was surprised at the question. "Well…I suppose. Though I hope you don't cramp my style."

Harper frowned. "Cramp your style? How could I do that?" Yes, fine, she knew her grandma had a better social life than she did, but how could she hold her back? Grandma did whatever she wanted, whenever she wanted to.

"I do have…friends. Of a…gentleman nature." Her grandma's lips screwed up into a little bright pink pout.

Harper kept her expression completely neutral. "I won't interfere with your dates. I promise."

"Not just dates." Grandma leaned over the table, her voice lowering to a whisper. "Sometimes I have sleepovers too."

Oh. She really tried not to look too scandalized, but she could feel her eyes growing wider. The last thing she wanted to think about was her grandma um…yeah. She couldn't even go there in her own head. "Well, if you're worried about me cramping your style, maybe I could stay at the condo?"

"Weston Gallagher lives there now, remember?" Grandma smiled.

No, Harper didn't remember because no one had mentioned that he was the new resident in her grandma's condo by the lake. "I didn't know," she mumbled.

"Oh, yes. He promised he'd fix the place up too. Nothing I like more than a man who's good with his hands."

Harper's cheeks went hot. West was very good with his hands. She could personally testify to that statement. She couldn't believe he lived there. She'd stayed at the condo before she moved in with Roger, so was he sleeping in her old bed, too? Most likely.

She hadn't seen West since the Forks Bar a few nights ago. They'd flirted a little bit, but once Tate entered the bar, he'd monopolized West for the rest of the evening.

They'd talked about work, and though at one point she'd sworn West looked a little pained over whatever they were chatting about, overall he and Tate seemed to get along just fine.

And for whatever reason, that had driven Wren crazy. She'd muttered about it to Harper the entire night, watching her brother and Tate far too closely. Harper noticed Tate kept looking over at them, offering up a sexy smile, his gaze only for...

Wren.

There was definitely something brewing between Wren and Tate, though Harper had no idea why Wren was fighting it so hard. Had Harper been so wrapped up in her own boring relationship she hadn't noticed that her best friend and Tate had some sort of thing going on? Why hadn't Wren ever mentioned it to her before? Why weren't they *acting* on it? If Harper had a guy as hot as Tate salivating over her and she was single, she'd go for it, no question. Wren wasn't attached and neither was Tate. So what was the big deal?

She swore she was going to find out. And soon.

"I'm guessing since West won't be there much, what with work and all, maybe you could ask him if he needs a roommate. Then you could take the guest bedroom. What do you think?" her grandma asked.

Horror filled Harper and she furiously shook her head. She thought her grandma had straight lost her mind, that's what. "Um, absolutely not. I can't move in with West. That's...crazy."

"Why? He's only there half the time and once the fire season really kicks into gear, he probably won't be there hardly ever," Grandma pointed out. "Hmm, I do hope he's going to work on the condo before he gets too wrapped up in fighting fires."

What her grandma was suggesting was ludicrous. She couldn't even begin to wrap her head around the idea of living with West. Spending lots of time with him, seeing him during private, intimate moments: West fresh out of the shower, a towel wrapped around his hips and his skin still damp. Or West first thing in the morning, his dark hair a mess, his eyes sleepy as he shuffled into the kitchen in search of coffee.

Hmm. Maybe she *could* imagine it. That was the problem.

"Living with West is out of the question," Harper finally said, glancing down at her empty coffee cup. "I need a job, too, Grandma. Just something temporary until I can—"

Her grandma cut her off, resting a hand to her chest, her bright red nails flashing as she said, "Oh, thank the Lord above. I thought you were going to continue working for Roger and that just wouldn't *do*, Harper. Not at all."

"You're right, I know. I just…I couldn't do it. I need to find something else."

She was here on a Wednesday morning. Roger had given her the week off—paid of course—so she could go in search of another job. But they were so few and far between in Wildwood. Maybe she could wait tables at the BFD until something better came along. Not that she was especially good at waiting tables, but a girl had to make money to live.

And Roger understood. He always understood. While at one point in their relationship she'd found his intuitive ways nurturing, so reaffirming of his love, after a while, it had just started to grate on her nerves. Why hadn't he ever yelled? Gotten mad? He had one mood and it was always the same: Calm. Even. Unruffled. In certain situations, it came in handy. But other times, she wanted more. She wanted...

Passion. It always came back to that.

"Of course you couldn't continue working for him. Now you're going to work for me."

Harper blinked at her grandmother, remaining silent. This was exactly what she wanted, but she'd figured she'd have to ask for the job.

"If I could give you one bit of relationship advice, I'd say never allow the man you're dating to be in a position of power over you. Roger was your *boss*."

Grandma shook her head, her gaze going hazy like it did when she was reminiscing. "I never dated a man I worked for. Not like I've worked many jobs in my life, to be truthful. But did you know that crazy old coot Buster Boner tried to hit me up about a year after your grandpa passed? He approached me at one of those Friday Nights at the Lake events and told me he had seventy-five thousand dollars in savings and two tickets to Hawaii—was I in?"

Her grandma changed subjects as quickly as the wind shifted on a particularly hot day in Wildwood.

"Were you in for what?" Harper vaguely remembered Buster Boner. First, because really, who could forget that

completely unforgivable and horrendous name? Buster
was a nickname—he'd actually chosen to be called that
versus whatever his real name was. He'd been a part of
her grandma's social circle back when Harper was a teen-
ager and he was quite the storyteller.

"He wanted to *take care of me*." Grandma made quota-
tion marks in the air with her fingers. "Saw me as a helpless old widow I guess. Thought he'd win me over with
an exotic trip and oodles of money." Grandma shook her
head, made a disapproving noise. "Men. They're ridiculous. Or they're wonderful. Take your pick."

Harper laughed. "They're all of those things. I completely agree."

"Of course you do. Now." Grandma slid out of the
booth and clapped her hands once. Her signal that meant
she was getting down to business. "Let me show you what
I'd like you to do for me here at the BFD."

Harper followed suit, frowning as she stood. "I
thought I would just be a waitress?" The very last thing
she wanted to be. Maybe she could be the cashier instead?
Or the hostess? Though the BFD never had someone who
was strictly the hostess. God, she didn't know what she
was going to do.

"Oh, goodness *no*. You're too qualified for that. I'm
going to let you into my inner sanctum, you lucky girl."
Her grandma started walking toward the back of the restaurant, but Harper remained rooted to the floor.

The inner sanctum was code for her grandma's office.
She never let anyone back there. It was forbidden. She had
her own filing system—total chaos—and if anyone came

in and toppled over one of the piles of receipts or folders or whatever, that was it. Her grandma went into a full-blown tizzy, shooing them out and barricading the door.

So everyone just stayed out of her office. It was easier that way.

When Harper still hadn't followed her grandma turned, glaring at her. "Come on now. I don't have all day."

"Um, why do you want me to go to your office?" Harper asked nervously.

Grandma had a look on her face that clearly said *duh*. "Because I want you to eventually take over the business, my darling girl. No one else could run this place but me—or you. And besides"—she grinned—"I have over two hundred thousand in the bank and I plan on buying two tickets to Hawaii. I'm going to need some time trying to size up which old coot I want to take along with me when I retire once and for all."

"I'M FUCKING STARVING," West muttered under his breath as he hopped out of the fire engine and slammed the door. The rest of his shift team joined him at the back of the engine and they all headed toward the entrance of the restaurant together as one.

This was his last full day on shift. Tomorrow morning at eight, he'd be off. It had been a productive four days, learning the routine of his new station, getting everyone's names straight, quietly figuring out who could possibly be trouble and who was a solid member of his team. So far, no one seemed to be much trouble. But it was still early in the fire season yet—Memorial Day weekend had only just passed—and all of them had been on their best behavior.

He could smell the tantalizing scent of burgers as far as the parking lot and his stomach growled in answer. They'd been going at it steadily since six this morning. Menial calls, every one of them, but just enough to keep them busy and unable to eat a real meal. He'd scarfed down a protein bar around ten and had a bottle of water with him always, but he was down-to-the-bones hungry.

And he was dying for a burger basket special from the BFD. When was the last time he came to this place? He couldn't remember. The Bigfoot Diner opened when he was still in high school, and at first he and his friends had done nothing but make fun of the place. Until they all went in together one night and tried the food out, only to discover it was mouthwateringly delicious.

They quit making fun of it after that.

Besides, he'd heard a rumor that Harper was working here and he was hoping to catch a glimpse of her. Totally juvenile of him, he knew, but he really was craving a BFD burger. They were the best in town.

"Do you eat here much?" West asked no one in particular. He knew one of them would eventually pipe up.

"I'm not much of a meat eater," Tori sniffed. The lone female firefighter on his crew, he liked Tori. Thank Christ she wasn't a newbie. They were too antsy and ready for action, like overeager puppies. Though she did have a stick up her butt half the time. Not that he could blame her. The guys were brutal. He used to be too, but now that he had to manage the crew? He was their leader and couldn't blow it by making some offhand remark.

"Yeah, we've heard that," one of the bozos said right before he started to crack up, but he was the only one laughing. Jon was his name. Cocky, mouthy, good-looking, and young, *he* was a newbie and the son of someone in the human resources department at headquarters, which made his attitude that much worse.

In other words, West couldn't stand the nineteen-year-old little asshole.

"Better watch your mouth," West said, his low tone warning enough. Jon's lips snapped shut and he sent a look to the other guys standing nearby. West turned away, not really caring if he pissed the kid off or not. He had a crew to run.

More like he had a crew to feed.

West pushed through the front door, Tori directly behind him, the rest of the crew falling into line after her.

They'd shed their turnouts earlier, after they'd fought a small vegetation fire started by a car flying off the road and landing in an empty cattle field. The hot transmission had lit the tall, dry grass beneath the car and within seconds more than an acre was burning. They got the fire out quick, but they were lucky the air still held a hint of moisture. Come late July into August, forget it. It would be dry as a bone.

He had to savor these days while he still had them. Predictions for this summer's fire season were off the charts. What with California suffering through a major drought, the conditions were ripe for most of the state to burn right up. The forest that surrounded Wildwood was dotted with dying trees, the lush green pines broken up by more and more brown trees as time went on. If they didn't have a wet winter with plenty of rain and snow soon, the entire forest was likely to die.

And then burn up.

A cute waitress approached, greeting them with a bright smile and an overenthusiastic hello. Her green T-shirt with the Bigfoot Diner logo emblazoned on the front stretched tight over her tits and he swore her nipples were hard. West did his best not to look at her chest, but the other guys were blatantly checking her out and practically drooling. Not that she seemed to mind.

Christ, he felt like an old man with this bunch.

"You want to sit outside or at a table in here?" the blonde waitress chirped at him, waving a hand at the remaining empty tables. Most everyone was sitting outside on the patio, enjoying the warm weather.

"Inside's fine." They needed to cool off and the restaurant's air-conditioning felt amazing. They all settled at a large table that could seat at least ten, most of them not bothering to look at a menu, West included.

He knew exactly what he wanted. Burger basket, no onions with a side of the special fry sauce that wasn't advertised. Only locals knew about it. Funny, how he'd fallen into his local routine pretty much the moment he'd stepped back into Wildwood.

"So what made you leave this place? I figured all Gallaghers were lifers when it came to Wildwood," Tori said to him after the waitress took everyone's order.

West was surprised by her question. Was she a mind reader or what? Didn't much like being called a lifer either. "I was offered a promotion so I took it," he said slowly, refusing to comment on the lifer part. "Why do you ask?"

As discreetly as he could possibly be, he let his gaze slide around the room in search of Harper, but she was nowhere in sight. He thought it was kind of odd, her possibly working at the diner. Didn't she work with her boyfriend? Hadn't she left to go to college for a few years? Hell, why hadn't she just flat out left for good? That's what he'd done though here he was, back where he started.

Harper was too damn good for this town.

Tori shrugged. "I know Holden, and he's mentioned you a few times. How you left Wildwood as fast as you could." When West still hadn't said anything she continued, "Holden and I were stationed together our first year. We went to the academy together."

All firefighters had to go to the academy before they were assigned to a station. If they failed, they couldn't become firefighters. It was hard enough to get into Cal Fire. Nothing worse than getting through the first gate only to be sent home packing because you couldn't pass the basic physical tests.

West had just finished up at the academy near Sacramento a few weeks ago. It was a requirement for his promotion—the engineer was the one who drove the fire engine and he had to pass the driver's test. Talk about sweating bullets. He'd practiced taking the test again and again, knocking over fewer and fewer cones with every try. Managing to squeeze that big-ass engine between the strategically placed orange cones hadn't been easy.

But he'd passed. Still felt damn good just thinking about it too.

"So you and Holden are friends?" West didn't think Holden could be friends with someone of the opposite sex, especially someone as naturally pretty as Tori, what with her long dark hair and warm brown eyes. But maybe considering he was so happy, so solid with Kirsten, Holden didn't even notice Tori.

Yeah right.

"Sort of. We don't really see each other much anymore except in passing." Tori sent him a meaningful look. "Are you happy to be back here?"

"I guess?" West hadn't meant for it to sound like a question, but he really wasn't sure how he felt about being in Wildwood. His father hadn't seemed thrilled at his return and he figured the old man would give him endless crap for coming back. So far, they hadn't talked much.

Just the way West liked it.

"I think I get what you mean. There's nothing to do here. I'm not even from this silly little town." Tori shrugged, casting her gaze about the restaurant with a critical eye. "I mean, really. A Bigfoot-themed restaurant? How lame can we get?"

"They have the best fucking burgers in town. Hands down," Jon said firmly, interrupting their conversation like he'd been listening the entire time. Nosy little fucker. "So quit your complaining. It's not our fault you're a vegetarian."

"Lay off," West said to Jon, his tone a warning. Though he couldn't believe what Tori said. Who knocked the BFD? Granted, the walls were covered in various Bigfoot sightings articles and even the metal napkin holders had a Bigfoot-walking silhouette on top of them, but it was Rebecca Hill's restaurant, one that she'd created in her late husband's honor. No one from Wildwood mocked the place.

Hell, even the tourists loved it. The place was packed, even at two in the afternoon.

Tori sent Jon a condescending look before turning toward West, a smile curling her lips. "I'm not really a vegetarian. I just don't eat beef."

He could really not care less about her eating habits, but it was noted just the same. They all took their turn cooking. Now he knew not to expect a juicy steak on Tori's kitchen shift. "Got it. No beef."

Her voice dropped and she leaned in close. "I heard there was a fire a few nights ago that was possible arson." She paused, her eyes meeting his. "Is it true?"

West knew nothing about it. And even if he did, he wouldn't discuss it like two kids gossiping in the cafeteria at school. "I only just got here so I don't know." He shrugged.

She breathed deep, glancing around. "I overheard Tate talking about it. Maybe I was mistaken."

"Maybe." West tried his best to remain neutral and made a mental note to ask Tate. Deep down, he was immediately filled with worry. If it was true and there really was an arsonist in Wildwood, he needed to know about it. He didn't like the idea of his hometown at risk. The town was surrounded by towering pine trees, many of them dead or dying because of the ongoing drought. This place could go up in flames easily, putting everyone at risk.

"So. Is it true that Harper Hill broke up with her boyfriend?" Tori waggled her brows at West's confusion.

She knew how to change the subject whip-fast. And why was she suddenly bringing up Harper? He'd forgotten just how small the town was. Everyone knew each other, even if only in passing.

"Talk about gossip," she said. "They were solid. Everyone thought they were getting married. Figured you'd have the lowdown on what happened, considering Harper's best friend is your sister."

"Harper and I aren't that close anymore." Kissing-close, but that was years ago and didn't count any longer. "I know nothing." Even if he did, that would be his automatic defense. No way would he spread any rumors or speculation about Harper. "What do you know about the boyfriend?" He wanted to kick himself for even asking.

Tori's waggling brows stay up, like she was surprised by his question. "I don't know much about Roger. He was quiet and kept to himself. Harper's always friendly, but she never really reveals herself to anyone."

Odd. He remembered Harper as being overly friendly. But then again, he wasn't a stranger to this town like Tori, not really. He'd known Harper since she was little and felt like he knew everything about her, even when that wasn't the case. "We grew up together," he said carefully, not wanting to say too much. What if Tori really was a friend to Harper and she'd tell her everything he said? Forget that. Hell, he was walking on shaky ground just by asking about Roger the boring ex. "But we haven't really stayed in contact since I left."

"I heard you didn't stay in contact with *anyone* after you left."

He said nothing, could only figure Holden told Tori that, which seemed like a pretty intimate thing for his brother to tell some random chick he worked with.

When he said nothing more, Tori sighed and gave up a little more information. "Roger wasn't from around here either. He's an accountant, bought the old H&R Block a few years ago and started his own business. Good-looking in that bland, *I've made appearances in a Sears catalog* way, if you know what I mean."

Scarily enough, West knew exactly what she meant.

"Nice enough, but boring." Tori shrugged. "You don't know him?"

"I haven't been back here in years, remember?" West prodded.

"Yeah, Holden had mentioned that once or twice." Her cheeks were a little pink. "We used to talk a lot, but not so much anymore."

The waitress suddenly appeared with a tray of drinks, and West got distracted by his growling stomach and the promise that food would be coming soon. And once the burger baskets finally arrived, everyone was so ravenous all conversation was forgotten as they stuffed their faces.

It wasn't until he pushed his empty basket away and wanted to groan over all the food he ate that he finally looked around once more for Harper. But there was no sign of her. Damn it, was she really at the restaurant now? Because he swore he could feel her presence—and that was insane. He had no business going in search of her. He was on duty, for Christ's sake. Though everyone was still eating and the radio attached to his belt was quiet, indicating that there weren't any calls.

Stretching his arms above his head, he braced his hands behind his neck, going for nonchalance. He hadn't spotted her grandmother either. Maybe he should go ask if Harper was in.

Would he look too eager? Yeah, probably, but he sort of didn't care. He wanted to talk to her. See how she was doing. They'd been interrupted at the bar last Saturday night and they'd never really had a chance to reconnect.

He needed to change that. Was curious to see how she treated him without their friends or family around. It probably wasn't right, seeking her out, trying to get closer to her, what with her recent breakup, but he couldn't help himself. The urge to see her smile, smell her intoxicating scent, was strong.

Besides, a little flirtation never hurt anyone. Right?

Chapter Five

GRANDMA PEEKED HER head around the doorway. "Someone's out there asking for you."

Harper looked up from the paperwork she was trying to comb through. "Who could be looking for me here?"

Her grandma had already taken off.

Only twenty-four hours into her new job and Harper was already exhausted. And majorly confused. Her grandma definitely wasn't the best when it came to organizing things. There was no rhyme or reason to the haphazard filing system the woman had adopted since she first opened the diner. It was really a system that only Rebecca Hill understood. Yet she wanted her wrecked system cleaned up "in case I leave the restaurant to you one day." Direct quote. Or worse, if the IRS ever decided to conduct an audit.

She was already overwhelmed and she'd only gone through the top drawer of one filing cabinet. Numerous filing cabinets lined one wall of the small office. Plus there was a closet full of past paperwork that she'd need to go through as well.

She figured she'd bitten off more than she could chew, but no way was she admitting that to anyone. Instead she'd soldier on like she was so good at doing, never complaining.

With a weary sigh Harper stood, stretching her arms above her head, twisting to the left, then the right, her cramped muscles protesting. Her back hurt from being hunched over the file cabinet and her grandma's messy desk the last two days. Upon entering the office, she'd vowed to have the entire spot clean in two weeks, but Grandma only laughed. Other employees of the restaurant had bets on exactly how long it would take Harper to clean up "the inner sanctum"—and how long Harper would last at the BFD in general.

Despite her reputation for being hardworking, no one had any faith in her. And that stung. Was it because to the outside world, it looked like she'd given up on Roger?

Tilting her neck to one side, then the other, she heard the satisfying crack. She'd show every single one of them eventually. So maybe it would take a little longer than she originally planned. She wasn't a quitter. Fine, she quit her relationship and her job, but she'd had no choice. If she hadn't shaken up her life, she'd have been in for years of the same thing, over and over again. Talk about boring. Maybe cleaning out her grandmother's office wasn't exactly the answer, but it was a start. However small.

She walked down the narrow hall past the bathrooms and the doorway to the kitchen until she was behind the diner's long counter, where mostly regulars sat for their midafternoon cup of coffee and piece of pie. The BFD served only Rebecca Hill's special homemade pie; it was famous throughout the region and both her lemon meringue and apple pies had won awards in the past.

When her grandma informed Harper last night she'd need to learn the recipes before she retired, Harper had almost experienced a full-blown panic attack. She wasn't much of a cook. And she definitely wasn't good at baking. How was she expected to take over the pie-making duties?

She smiled at old Lester Marcum, who nodded his greeting since his mouth was too stuffed with pie. Glancing around the restaurant, she spotted the group from Cal Fire, recognizing a few faces, though there was no Tate and he was the one who typically accompanied this particular group.

"There you are."

The familiar, deep warm voice came from directly behind her. She went still, closing her eyes briefly because she knew she looked an absolute mess and she didn't want to see *him* like this: not a lick of makeup on; her hair in the sloppiest knot on top of her head barely held together with a pen; she wore a faded BFD T-shirt that was dirty from her rummaging around in her grandma's dusty office; old denim shorts that were frayed at the hem; and beat-up white Converse that really weren't white at all, more like a nondescript gray that came from many years of wear.

Taking a deep breath, she opened her eyes and turned to face him, a firm smile on her face. She'd just pretend she was dressed up and looking gorgeous. *Fake it until you make it.* "Weston. Imagine running into you here." She should've known he would've brought the fire crew to the diner.

"I heard you were working at the BFD and had to see it for myself." He grinned, ridiculously good-looking in his navy blue uniform. She tried to keep her gaze focused on his face and not blatantly check him out, but she couldn't help herself.

She blatantly checked him out. And liked every single thing she saw too. She'd never been one to fall for a guy in a uniform. Never thought much about a guy in full military dress or some sexy uniformed cop—Wren went through a stage a few years ago where she was hot for every young cop in uniform she saw. Didn't help that her big brother had a swarm of various deputies for friends. They only fed her fantasy. But she got over it quick because Lane nipped it in the bud, saying none of his friends were worthy of dating her.

There was nothing like a big brother to put a major damper on his sister's not-so-secret fantasy.

Right now though, Harper was considering all sorts of fantasies involving West in his uniform. She especially liked the thick black utility belt he wore. The heavy boots on his feet. And those tattoos that covered his arms, those were new. Every single one of them. They were hot too. And mysterious. She wanted to know the meaning behind them all. Made her want to unbutton his uniform shirt slowly and reveal the T-shirt beneath. She had a feeling it clung to his every muscle just right…

"Does your grandma have you outside digging in the dirt or what?" West asked, pushing her out of her thoughts.

Harper blinked up at him. He must've seen the confusion on her face because he leaned in a little closer, his voice low as he said, "You're kind of dirty."

Ah, if he said that while implying a different, more scandalous meaning, she would be blushing. But she really was dirty. She glanced down at herself, wiping at the front of her shorts. More like absolutely filthy. "I'm cleaning out her office right now. It's sort of a nightmare."

He whistled low. "Sounds rough."

"Trust me, it is." Though nothing was as rough as fighting wildfires, going on medical calls, car accidents…all the stuff West did on a daily if not hourly basis. He probably thought she was a complete and total joke, griping about cleaning out a stupid file cabinet and getting paper cuts. But damn it, those little slices in her skin *hurt*. "How are you doing? Is your first shift back in Wildwood going well? Are we keeping you busy?"

"So far, it's been good." He glanced back at the table where the others from his station sat finishing their meals. "And today was extra busy. Finally got a chance to stop off for a late lunch."

"Well, we're honored you chose the BFD." She smiled, trying to fight the nerves bouncing in her stomach from the way West watched her so carefully. "How was your food?"

"Delicious, as usual." His gaze dropped to her lips, lingering there, and her lips tingled as if he'd reached out and physically touched them. She shouldn't react this way, right? She'd broken up with Roger only a few days ago and she was already having physical feelings for someone else. Granted, those feelings were for someone she'd harbored a secret crush on for years, but still. It was wrong.

Wrong, wrong, wrong.

"Good to hear it." Her smile wavered when his expression turned serious. Deadly serious. She had the sudden urge to run. "I, um, should let you get on with your afternoon, then. Take care, West."

She started to walk away, but he stopped her just by saying her name.

"Harper." She turned to face him again and he reached out, rubbing his thumb across her cheek, just beneath her eye. She sucked in a breath when he touched her, awareness prickling from his nearness, his fingers on her skin, however briefly. "You had dirt on your face," he explained.

"Oh," she said weakly. God, could she sound dumber? Her knees wobbled and she tried to smile at him but failed miserably. "Thanks." She went to move past him, but he stopped her again, his fingers circling her wrist.

"What are you doing tomorrow?" he asked.

Was he actually asking her out on a date? No freaking way. He hadn't let go of her wrist. Did he feel her pulse fluttering wildly under his fingers? Probably. And there was nothing she could do about it either. "Um, digging through piles of old receipts in my grandma's office?"

His eyes warmed, his lips curling into the faintest smile. "Sounds exciting. How about after you get off work?"

"Um." She swallowed hard, hating that she'd said *um* twice like some sort of idiot. *Don't blow this!* "Nothing, really."

"Want to come over? I was hoping I could get your input on something." When she sent him a puzzled look he continued. "Your grandma wants me to paint the interior walls at the condo. I had some other ideas of what I'm considering doing to the place, too, but I wanted to get your insight before I started."

"Oh." Disappointment wrapped her in its embrace, leaving her cold. She slowly withdrew her hand from his grip, giving him a tight smile. "Sure. I'd be glad to help you." It's what she did, after all. Helped people. Harper Hill, ever accommodating, always ready to lend a helpful hand. Even West realized this, but how could he not? That's what everyone expected from her. She wasn't wild and crazy, like Delilah. She wasn't opinionated, saying whatever the hell she wanted whenever she wanted, like Wren. She was quiet and accommodating and what the hell was that ever going to get her in life?

"Thanks, Harper. That would be great." He smiled, looking pleased. He just wanted to earn her grandma's approval for fixing up her place. This had nothing to do with her or him and what they shared so long ago. She was a fool to even think it.

"What time do you want me to come over?"

"What time are you done here?"

"Around five I guess?" Ugh, she didn't want to go over to his place at all. Not if he just wanted to show her paint samples and ask her opinion about tearing out the ugly brown tile in the downstairs bathroom—which she'd say yes to if he asked, and she really hoped he asked.

Yeah. She was ridiculous. Falling right into helpful mode even in her thoughts like she couldn't stop herself, which she supposed she couldn't. Not like she could talk about her problems with Wren and Delilah either. Wren would freak out if she knew Harper was hot for her big brother. And Delilah was West's ex-girlfriend so no way was she broaching the subject with her. For all she knew, Delilah was still interested in West.

Though deep down, Harper suspected Delilah was really lusting for Lane Gallagher. But that was another story for another time.

"Call me when you're done." His gaze shifted to the top of her head. "Gonna borrow this."

He pulled the pen from her hair, causing it to fall past her shoulders in haphazard, totally weird waves. If she didn't curl it, she straightened her hair every morning. Seeing it in its natural state wasn't a good thing and she was quietly mortified West did just that.

"Let me give you my cell number."

He took her hand and flipped it over, writing his phone number on her palm like they were in still in school. She tucked her hair behind her ear with her free hand, hoping it didn't look too awful. Praying he wouldn't notice the subtle tremor running just beneath her skin.

"How old are we again?" she teased.

West glanced up at her through his absurdly long eyelashes, his gaze meeting hers. "Sorry. I just wanted to make sure you had a way to contact me." He paused, appearing a little unsure. A look she wasn't used to seeing West wear. "You'll call when you're done here tomorrow?"

"I'll call you. Or I'll text," she reaffirmed, wondering if maybe he *was* interested in her. Maybe this was more than talking about paint color and redoing the countertops?

"Good." The relief on his face was evident. "You look really pretty with your hair down, Harper. You should wear it like that more often."

And with that he was gone, headed back to the table where his crew waited for him, more than a few of them eyeing her curiously.

Blushing like a fool, she hurried out of the dining area, back to the sanctuary of her grandma's office, where she could relive the words Weston Gallagher just said to her about her stupid, crazy hair.

"So, HEY."

Later that afternoon, West turned to find Tate and…Lane? Standing in front of him.

"We want to talk to you," Tate said, his expression serious, though no one did serious like his big brother. He had the look down pat.

Lane stood just behind Tate, scowling at him as they waited for his response. He didn't say a damn word. That had always been his best defense tactic and it worked for him.

West scratched the back of his head with one hand while pulling out a chair with the other. They were in the kitchen, the only ones in there. Everyone else was outside washing the engines. West was about to bail since he was off shift, thankful to head back to his condo, where he'd collapse into his bed—or what he liked to think of as Harper's old bed—and sleep like the dead for a few hours.

Instead, he was sitting across from his big brother and his captain, unable to shake the feeling that he was in trouble. Old habits died hard.

"What's up?" he asked, hoping like hell he sounded casual.

Tate looked at Lane, who nodded as if in approval before Tate started to talk. "We didn't want to bring it up around the others, but…we're fairly certain there's an arsonist in the area."

Unease slipped down his spine. He recalled his earlier conversation with Tori. Guess her speculation was based in truth after all. "What makes you say that?"

"It started earlier this spring," Tate said, leaning forward so his forearms rested on the table between them. "Had a few spotty fires here and there. No big deal at first. Most of them seemed accidental. They were always put out pretty fast and we were thankful they didn't turn into more. Yet they kept happening, so after a bit of investigating, prevention discovered they were all started by the same accelerant. And it was too coincidental to be an accident."

West glanced over at Lane, who was wearing his neutral *I'm a cop* face. It was also really close to his irritating

I'm your big brother so you have to listen to me or else face. Both sucked. "How are you involved in this?"

"When prevention can't make it, they call in the sheriff's department." Lane sent him a look, one that said he should know this. Maybe West did, maybe he didn't. It still felt good to question Lane, which was stupid. He really needed to get rid of this big brother–shaped chip on his shoulder.

"So have there been any fires so far this year?" West asked.

"We think that vegetation fire yesterday was related," Lane stated, but West shook his head emphatically.

"No way. That's impossible. I was there, first on scene. Simple fire started by a hot car engine."

"It flared back up," Tate said, his tone and expression grim. "Last night, when you were on the call with that truck that rolled off the side of the road, the call went out and we responded. There was no reason for that fire to start again. None. Luckily enough someone who lived on the road was driving home and spotted it. Otherwise, it could've grown quickly and done some major damage."

West silently agreed. They'd put the fire out fast. The burned hulk of metal that used to be a car was towed out of the field within the hour. The mop-up had been simple and quick. Fire out. Case closed.

"We found the same accelerant as from the ones last summer. They're using paint thinner," Lane added. "Someone went back out there and purposely set another fire to make it look like the old fire had flared back up. It was pretty easy to figure out when we went back to the scene."

None of them said another word, but West would bet money they were all thinking the same thing. So many arsonists were volunteers. Frustrated men and women who wanted to be firefighters but couldn't get hired on at a department no matter how hard they tried. So they lit the fires and were first on the scene, trying to look like heroes. In a few instances, some arsonists were also fire-fighters, captains, whatever. Hell, there was that one guy who was an actual arson investigator and had lit up all of Southern California for years. Once he was arrested and tossed in jail, the fires in the area reduced dramatically.

"Could it be…one of us?" West asked hesitantly. "Not one of *us* specifically, but you know what I mean."

"We've thought about it," Tate said, "though we haven't questioned anyone yet. Hell, we haven't even announced our suspicions. No media outlets have been notified. No one knows. We were hoping to solve the problem quickly, but I think we're going to have to take this public. Before it gets out of hand." Tate sighed, look-ing frustrated. "But for right now, we need you to keep this strictly confidential."

"No one else can know," Lane emphasized. "We're only telling you because I told Tate we could trust you."

"Gee, thanks," West muttered sarcastically, causing Lane to glare at him.

"You know what I mean," Lane said, shaking his head, completely irritated. West always knew just how to get under his brother's skin. "Just keep an eye out. If you see anything let one of us know. But remember, we also need your silence."

"I don't know if my silence will matter much, considering people are talking." At their frowns, West continued, "Someone from my crew mentioned it to me earlier."

"We'll have to tell them something eventually, but for now, let's keep it quiet," Lane said, his voice grim.

"A lot to heap on you at the end of your first shift here," Tate said with a faint smile.

"Technically it's not my first shift here," West said. They talked like he was some sort of idiot. "I was stationed here my first season as a firefighter." And he didn't want Tate to forget it. He may be the captain, but West had been here first. He was the one with Wildwood in his blood. No matter how much he tried to deny it, it was true. He was born and raised here. This town belonged to him. And now someone threatened it.

Even though he didn't work in prevention, he would do his damnedest to help figure out who that person was. Whatever it took.

HIS EARLIER PLAN of sleeping most of the day away went to shit after his meeting with Lane and Tate. They both pulled the asshole *we're more in charge than you* attitude on him after they were finished discussing the supposed arsonist. Their matching behavior had irritated West so much he'd bailed on the station quick, hightailing it back to his place, where he ended up sprawled across the couch, TV remote in hand as he watched a bunch of bullshit daytime television.

That stuff was the worst.

But he did stumble upon a documentary on one of those crime channels about, of all things, an arsonist. A young guy who tried to burn up most of the industrial buildings in a Washington town back in the nineties. West had watched the entire show with interest, paying attention to the behavior of the arsonist, even taking notes on the reasons behind it. The psychologist's conclusions?

The dude had daddy issues.

What a bunch of shit.

West dozed on the couch, his sleep fitful, as the living room grew warmer and warmer with the early summer sun shining hot and intense outside. But he was too lazy to get up and turn on the air conditioner. He needed to take a shower. Harper was coming over tonight and he wanted to look his best…

Springing into a sitting position, West scrubbed his hair back, glancing around for his phone. He found it, and checked the time, realizing quickly that most of the afternoon had gone by. Shit, he had to take a shower, figure out what the hell he was going to wear. He wanted to look good but not like he'd tried too hard.

Why did he care so much what he was wearing for his meeting tonight with Harper anyway? Had he turned into a girl over the last twenty-four hours? He reminded himself of Wren—meaning that he was being freaking ridiculous.

Still, maybe he could take Harper out to dinner afterward. If they went somewhere in Wildwood though, that might be a mistake. Like waving a red banner for everyone in town to see: he and Harper were out on an actual date. He could hear the locals now.

Hmm. That's moving pretty fast, especially for Harper Hill. And so soon after her breakup with poor, lonely Roger? How could she?

Oh yeah, Wildwood residents would have a field day over that one.

Scratch any dinner plans then. They'd either have to order in or he'd have to make her something, and the last thing he wanted to do was cook.

His mom had called earlier, asking if he wanted to come over for dinner, but he'd declined. Her disappointment was palpable, even over the phone, though she really didn't say much. And of course, he'd ended up feeling guilty. He knew his mom wanted to reconnect—his dad, he wasn't so sure, but Mom, most definitely. And he wanted to reconnect too. It was just so damn hard. He still harbored some resentment. Some worry.

Some fears.

That they wouldn't accept him, that his father would give him endless shit like usual, comparing him with his brothers like he loved to do. That was the last thing he needed.

Irritated with himself, West ran up the stairs two at a time and nearly stumbled on the top step like a dumbass. He then headed into the bathroom and practically tore the towel rack off the wall as he pulled the thick gray towel off so he could throw it over the shower door. If he kept this up, the condo would crumble around his ears.

No wonder Rebecca Hill had given him such a good deal on the rent in exchange for fixing the place up.

The place desperately needed some quality TLC.

He took a shower, scrubbed himself clean as fast as possible, his phone sitting on the edge of the counter, mocking him with its silence. He burst from the steamy shower the moment he turned off the water, dripping all over the tile floor as he grabbed his phone to check the time and see if he'd received a message yet.

Ten after five and zero messages.

He plucked a brand-new razor from its packaging, lathered up his face, and shaved. He'd slapped enough aftershave on his cheeks to know they felt baby soft and smooth. He combed his hair, wondered if he should get a haircut or leave it alone for now. Saw a wrinkle beside his right eye and proceeded to examine it for way too long.

Still there was no text from Harper.

West brushed his teeth and flossed—his dentist would probably faint from glee at seeing him do this. He swished a capful of mouthwash, wincing and grimacing, almost sputtering when he finally spit it out. He rubbed a hand across his chest and wondered if he should shave the hair off there. Or maybe get it waxed?

A shudder moved through him. He'd seen *The 40-Year-Old Virgin*. No way was he getting that shit waxed. Some women seemed to prefer the smooth look, but if Harper did? Tough shit. He wasn't shaving the hair off his chest or belly for a woman, not even one as pretty and delicious as Harper Hill.

And now he'd moved into full-on ridiculousness mode. Considering waxing his fucking chest, for the love of God. Staring at his reflection in the mirror and contemplating every single flaw he currently had. He'd straight up lost his damn mind. All over a girl.

A very special girl, he could admit, but still.

A special and increasingly annoying girl who still hadn't texted him. It was driving him crazy.

He grabbed a pair of black boxer briefs but didn't slip them on yet. He was letting the boys air out first after a particularly hot shower. Naked, he went through his meager belongings, dismissing every single thing he owned. Finally he threw on a pair of khaki cargo shorts and a black T-shirt. He was putting too much thought into this and he never did that. Keeping it simple was the name of the game.

West needed to remember that. When Harper arrived—and she would arrive, he knew this—he needed to act cool and calm. Composed. Behaving like an antsy, unsure idiot wasn't the way to keep Harper's interest.

Not by a long shot.

His phone buzzed. He heard the vibration send the iPhone jittering across the tiled bathroom countertop. Grabbing it, he was glad when he saw the unknown number, the words that accompanied it.

So. I'm done with work and I'm completely filthy. Do you mind if I take a shower first before I come over?

West fought the weird feeling washing over him. The one that was utter relief combined with—was that happiness? *Giddiness?* He didn't do giddy. He was a man, for the love of God. Men didn't get giddy.

I approve of filthy.

The moment he sent the text he worried. Would she be offended by his remark? He always remembered Harper having a pretty easygoing nature and a sharp sense of humor but he didn't want to upset her. Not when he was trying to work his way back in her good graces.

You would, you big perv. ☺

More relief flooded him.

Take your shower. Text me before you leave your house.

A few minutes ticked by and he was suddenly nervous. It was so insane he felt that way, about Harper of all people. But she'd always managed to get under his skin.

I'm staying at my grandma's. It'll take me five minutes to get to your place. If that.

He didn't want to appear too anxious, but…he wanted her here. Now.

Text me when you leave your grandma's house anyway. Just so I know.

Will do. ☺

She liked emojis. Smiley faces. He liked that about her. There were a lot of things he liked about Harper. Many things that had kept him up at night since his return to Wildwood. Hell, if he was being truthful with himself, he'd thought about her a lot even when he hadn't been in Wildwood. The one night they'd shared hadn't been enough. Not be a long shot.

So what he was going to do with all those old memories and current thoughts, dirty ones and all? That he wasn't so sure of.

Chapter Six

THE DOOR SWUNG open within seconds of Harper knocking on it, her hand still hovering in the air. West stood in the doorway, looking fresh and clean and stupid gorgeous in a pair of cargo shorts and a black T-shirt that stretched across his broad chest in the most fascinating way.

Harper took a step back, needing the space. *Oh, boy.* How was she going to concentrate on not throwing herself at him when he looked like that?

"Hey." He smiled, looking completely at ease and comfortable in his skin. How she envied that. She was nothing but restless energy and a bundle of nerves. "Glad you made it."

West held the door open wider and she walked inside, the familiar smell of her former home now filled with the unbelievably delicious scent that was Weston Gallagher.

As discreetly as possible she inhaled, keeping her back to him as he closed the door.

Soap. Man. Spicy. Clean. He was her new favorite fragrance.

"Tough day at work?" he asked, stopping directly beside her.

She glanced up at him, appreciating the fact that he was so tall. Roger was average height. Most of the guys she'd dated weren't especially tall. But West towered over her, her head barely meeting his shoulder. He made her feel small. Feminine.

"Brutal," she said. "I plowed my way through receipts that were dated back to 2004."

"That's over ten years ago," he pointed out.

"Wow, you're a mathematician master," she said with a somber nod, making him laugh.

"Not even close. I failed geometry and had to take summer school as a redo." He made a face. "Worst summer of my life."

Harper silently called bullshit on that statement. She'd lived that moment in time, had spent most of her days and nights at the Gallagher house. That was the summer West and Delilah got together. She'd been retaking geometry too and they were in class together, but whatever. No way did Harper want to bring that little fact up.

"I spent most of the afternoon shredding all of those receipts. You don't have to keep them that long for tax purposes, though my grandma sure thought so," Harper explained.

"I'm guessing you found older receipts too?"

"I haven't found them—yet. But she confirmed they're waiting for me in boxes in a storage unit she has just outside of town." Harper grimaced and West chuckled again. It was a nice sound, if a bit rusty. She had a feeling he didn't laugh much, and that was a shame.

"Want one of the engines to come in and help you? Start a controlled burn with all those boxes?" he asked. "Might be easier than shredding everything." Clearly he was joking, but she was tempted to take him up on the offer.

"It would probably get out of control quick, and we can't have that." She made a little face and he smiled, his gaze warm and making her insides tap dance with giddiness. This felt like flirting and she so didn't want to get her hopes up. But when it came to West, it was like she couldn't help herself.

She needed to focus and stay on task. There was a purpose for her visit tonight and it had nothing to do with flirting. "So. Where are the paint samples?"

West frowned, like he didn't know what she was talking about.

"You know, the reason why you asked me over here in the first place?" she added.

"Right. Yeah." He turned and went into the kitchen, Harper following after him. A pile of various paint samples from Home Depot sat on the counter and he picked them up, handing them to her. "What's your favorite color?"

"Well, it depends on the room." She set the pile on the counter and flipped open the first pamphlet to find it featured nothing but varying shades of white. Frowning, she scanned the different-color swatches. Who knew there were this many types of white in the world?

"What do you mean?"

Harper looked up at him, telling herself not to fall for the adorably confused look on his face. She really hated how much she wanted to give in to her West-based urges. "Well, different rooms should be painted different colors. Just because I love sea foam green doesn't mean I want my living room painted sea foam green, you know what I mean?"

His frown deepened. "What the hell is sea foam green?"

He was such a man. She held back the urge to roll her eyes. "A hideous color I don't really like."

"Then why would you suggest it?"

Sighing, she gathered up the paint samples and took them with her to the tiny kitchen table, where she sat down. "Sorry. Bad example. Come sit with me."

He did as she asked, pulling his chair right up next to hers, which proved to be completely distracting within seconds. His arm brushed hers as he reached over to grab a sample—the nothing-but-white one—and she could smell him. Feel the warmth emanating from his skin. Hear him shift and move and *breathe*, for the love of God. All simple things. He wasn't trying to drive her out of her mind with lust, but he so was.

And she was ridiculous for feeling this way.

"Well, all the rooms should probably be repainted, but I think your grandma wanted the kitchen worked on first. She mentioned she wanted new appliances, but I think she might want to wait before she makes that purchase," he explained.

Harper propped her elbow on the table and rested her chin on her fist, listening to him. She could listen to him all night, even when he talked about boring stuff like appliances and repainting. Not that she didn't want to help him, because she definitely did. But he was a total distraction. His deep voice, his gorgeous face, those sexy blue eyes, the way his broad chest was emphasized in that black T-shirt...

"So the cabinets are solid, but that oak is just so dark, it looks pretty beat up from years of use. I want to paint them white." He stared at the array of white samples with a helpless expression. "I thought it would be simple, you know? White is...white."

Hmm, she needed to step in and help him make a decision. She was good at this sort of thing. "Clearly that's not the case." She reached over and tapped her finger right in the dead center of about twenty white paint options. "I like this."

West glanced up. "Why's that?"

"I like the name. Café au Lait." She shrugged when he turned to really look at her, his blue eyes meeting hers. "It's not too bright, not too beige. It's a perfect, subtle shade of warm white."

"I like the way you think. Done." He tore the page out of the pamphlet, then proceeded to tear the actual paint sample itself from the page. "How about the kitchen walls?"

And that became their process. She declared a color as her favorite for a particular room and West agreed, no questions asked. He'd make jokes, and she couldn't help but laugh. He asked about people they went to school with, and she filled him in on whatever details she knew, which most of the time were a lot. He was a gracious host who kept asking her if she wanted something to drink until she finally agreed to have a bottled water. When he admitted he was hungry and she agreed, he called in a pizza order. They were waiting for it as he showed her the master bathroom, though she didn't really need a tour of the place.

She had lived here for years, after all.

"The tile has to go," West said as he flicked on the bathroom light. It was an old rectangular fluorescent unit that hung above the mirror, the light it cast dull and unflattering. If she had her choice, most everything in this room would go. It was all outdated and awful.

Harper stopped just behind him, her upper lip curling as she stared at the hideous brown tile that looked like it had come straight out of the seventies. "I totally agree. Shit brown isn't what I would call a classic color."

His gaze met hers in the bathroom mirror, his expression mildly incredulous. "Excuse me, but did Harper Hill just say the word *shit*?"

"Stop." She waved a hand. She'd had a bit of a reputation when she was younger as someone who never, ever cursed. Like ever. She'd been such a good girl back in her teenage years and so proud of it too.

Now she wished she would've gone a little wilder. At least once, just to prove that she could.

"Seriously. You don't say bad words, Harper. I don't know if I've ever heard you say the word *shit* and I've known you a long time." His face was serious, but she saw the way his eyes sparkled. He was totally teasing her.

"Well, it's been years since we've spent any time together. I've changed a lot, you know," she pointed out.

His gaze did a slow sweep of her body, lingering on all the spots that made her tingle in anticipation. "I can see that," he drawled.

In the mirror, her cheeks were pink. Some things never changed—like how she blushed at the drop of a hat. "I curse all the time," she mumbled.

"For real?" He sounded like he didn't believe her.

"Absolutely. *Shit* is my favorite word." She lifted her chin, trying to look dignified, but really, she was being an idiot.

This was what she'd been reduced to while in West's presence. She insisted that she loved to say bad words and that *shit* was her favorite.

Could she be any dumber?

"*Shit* is a good word, I have to agree." He moved closer to her, his long fingers trailing along the edge of the ugly countertop. She remembered exactly what it felt like to have those fingers trailing on her skin and she wanted to experience that again. "But I have other favorites."

"You do?" Her voice went higher and she cleared her throat, mentally reminding herself to keep her, *ahem*, shit together.

"One in particular." West turned to face her and all the air lodged in her throat when she saw how dark his eyes had become, how close he was to her now. She should tell him to back off. They were moving too fast. She'd just broken up with her boyfriend, the man she had assumed she was going to marry.

Instead she gripped the edge of the counter with one hand, bracing herself, waiting for something, anything to happen. Hopeful. Always hopeful when it came to West.

"What word is it?" she asked, pleased that her voice didn't come out shaky. She certainly felt shaky, like a fluttering leaf about to get knocked off a branch during the height of fall.

He smiled and stepped closer, a wicked glint in his eyes. "Well. I've always been partial to the word *fu*—"

The doorbell rang, interrupting him, making her jump in surprise. Frustration rippled across his features and he stepped back, running a hand through his hair before he smiled weakly. "Guess that's the pizza. I'll go get it."

"Do you want some money?" she offered. "I can help…"

The look he sent Harper told her she just affronted his manhood. "Keep your money. It's a ten-dollar pizza." He exited the bathroom, calling over his shoulder, "Come down and join me. We'll eat at the kitchen table."

The moment he was headed downstairs she leaned against the counter, resting her hand on her chest, trying her best to calm her racing heart and recover her wits before she went to the kitchen and joined him.

He was definitely being flirty, but why? Was he just a tease? Yes. Yes, she knew that for a fact. So was he leading her along, playing with her because he had nothing better to do? When he'd been younger he'd done that sort of thing all the time with a variety of girls, including at one point, her. He had a bit of a reputation, so if he was trying to uphold it with his return to Wildwood, so far he was doing a great job.

Shaking her head, she stared at her reflection, her gaze stern, a scowl on her face. "Don't fall for him," she murmured, wagging her index finger at the mirror. "He's dangerous to your well-being."

Truer words were never spoken.

Too bad she wasn't listening to her own advice.

WEST TIPPED THE delivery kid ten bucks and snatched the pizza box from his hands.

"Thanks, mister!" the teenaged boy said just as West slammed the door in his face.

Yeah, that was a jerk move, but he doubted the kid cared. He just scored an easy ten bucks.

West took the pizza into the kitchen and set the box on the counter before he opened the fridge, pulling out two bottles of pale ale. He knew Harper hadn't been much of a beer drinker when they were younger and maybe she wasn't one now either. He could change out her drink. He had other options.

All he knew was *he* needed the beer to loosen up. Just having her close made him incredibly tense. Even doing something as innocent and boring as picking out paint colors. Being with her, listening to her voice, watching her as she nibbled on her lower lip while contemplating paint samples sent a white-hot bolt of lust straight through him. He wanted to touch. Taste. Kiss. Strip.

Fuck.

Breathing deep, he twisted the top off his beer and took a few chugs, then went in search of paper plates and napkins. A little brown paper bag full of Parmesan and red pepper flakes came with the delivery and he pulled out a bottle of ranch dressing from the fridge too, remembering how Harper used to like dunking her pizza in it.

Funny, he hadn't remembered that particular detail until this very moment.

"Oh, it smells amazing." She walked into the kitchen, coming to a stop when she saw the pizza box on the counter. "DeMarco's? I haven't had that in forever." It was a Wildwood staple, having been around since West could remember.

"Seriously?" He flipped open the box, his mouth watering as he gazed at the pizza within. Growing up, he'd loved DeMarco's pizza. Would occasionally dream about it over the years, which was insane, but that's how much he missed it once he moved away.

He'd had it twice since he'd returned home. This was his third go-round. If he kept this up he'd be fat as hell and have a permanent case of serious heartburn.

She stared down at the pizza with longing. Actual, real longing etched all over her pretty face. "I try to watch what I eat now," she admitted, her voice soft. A little sad.

West ran his gaze down the length of her. She looked perfectly fine to him. Too fine. Curves in all the right places, not too skinny, the type of body a man wanted to run his hands all over. "You look great to me."

Her gaze met his, her eyes wide, lips softly parted. Completely kissable, if he was being honest with himself. He was half tempted to lean in and test it out. See if they'd have that same spark. See if she'd push him away or not.

But he remained rooted to the spot, not moving a muscle, not saying a word.

"Well, thank you. But that's because I don't eat DeMarco's anymore." She reached for the smallest slice and set it on the paper plate he offered her. "I'll just have one."

"Harper, you used to eat this stuff all the time. What gives?" He grabbed three pieces and stacked them on his plate. "And I have ranch out for you if you want to use it."

"Oh, I can't do that either. Just extra calories." She shook her head and started to head for the table. His gaze zeroed in on the sway of her hips, the perfect curve of her ass. A few extra calories wouldn't hurt that very sexy body of hers. Who was filling her head with such lies?

"Want a beer? Or does that have too many calories too?" he asked.

She sent him an admonishing look from over her shoulder before she settled in at the table. "Just water, thanks."

Muttering under his breath, he grabbed her another bottle of water and brought everything over to the table, including the ranch dressing and the two beers he was now going to drink himself. He dumped a bunch of ranch on his plate then dunked his slice into it, taking a big bite.

Damn. He hadn't eaten pizza with ranch in a long time. It was delicious.

The look Harper sent him as he chewed was now filled with pure jealousy. She wanted the ranch dressing, so why wouldn't she just go for it? "Why are you depriving yourself?"

She nibbled on her tiny slice of pizza, like she was trying to prolong the moment. "If I ate whatever I wanted, whenever I wanted it, I'd be huge."

He snorted. "I doubt that."

"It's true. I've given up most junk food. I had to," she said defensively.

"Well, that's a damn shame. I get eating healthy. I prefer it most of the time. But sometimes, I want a burger basket from the BFD," he explained.

"Or a huge slice of DeMarco's pizza covered in ranch?" She raised her brows, nodding toward his plate.

"Exactly." He set the half-eaten slice on his plate and licked his fingers just to drive her nuts. The way her eyes narrowed, he figured his plan was working. "It's freaking delicious. You're missing out."

She made a face. "You're mean."

"You're the mean one, torturing yourself."

"Oh my God," she mumbled, reaching out and grabbing the ranch dressing bottle, twisting off the cap. "You're also ridiculous."

"Says the girl who thinks she's fat." It pleased him to watch her squeeze a small dollop of dressing on her plate.

She delicately dipped the end of her slice in the dressing and then ate it, her eyes going dreamy with pleasure.

His skin went hot. He liked that look. A lot. Even if it was initially caused by pizza and ranch, he'd like to be the one to put that look on her face eventually.

"You should have another piece," he suggested after she devoured the first one. Before she could say a word he got up, grabbed the pizza box from the kitchen, and brought it back to the table. He flipped open the box, waving a hand. "Go for it."

She sighed, then pressed her lips together. "Maybe just one more?"

"No judgment here," he said solemnly.

"I'll have to work out extra hard tomorrow to make up for this." She reached for a slice, grabbing a much bigger one this time around.

He could think of a workout that they could indulge in together to burn a bunch of calories. Not that Harper would take him up on the suggestion. Not that she should. She was still recovering from ending her relationship. He was looking for nothing serious. He'd be fling material, nothing more.

Maybe that was exactly what Harper needed…

"What do you do to work out?" he asked, genuinely curious. He remembered she'd been on the volleyball team in high school. Her freshman year she'd been a cheerleader and cute as absolute fuck in her uniform. Harper could wear a short skirt like no one else. Even Delilah and she had those long dancer legs. "Still play volleyball?"

Harper made a face. "No. I haven't played it in years."

Of course she didn't. And he never thought about Delilah like that anymore either. Yeah, they'd had a thing when they were kids. A pretty passionate thing, if he was being truthful. As passionate as two teenage kids could be. But it had fizzled out fast. They were better off as friends and had realized it quick, which was awfully grown-up for them. They'd been babies then.

Seeing Delilah now, there was no spark, no interest. More like a pleasant fondness and memories of a time past. He was hopeful that they could continue their friendship. Delilah was good people. She always had been.

Harper Hill was…different. Just hearing her name being said by someone else sent a bolt of sensation straight through his veins. Hearing her voice made his heart race. Having her so close, or worse, having her touch him, however briefly, however meaningless it was…

He felt weak—weak with wanting her.

Was it because he'd never had a real chance with her? One night of kissing for a few hours hadn't been nearly enough. More like a sampling of what he wanted more of. Once he had her—if he ever got the chance—would he get over this feeling? Or would that make him want her more?

For all he knew she wasn't interested in him like that. He couldn't blame her. He'd treated her like crap by walking away and never acknowledging what happened that night. Of course, he'd left town and never had the chance to talk about it with her, but maybe that had only made it worse.

Hell, he *still* hadn't acknowledged what happened between them. Maybe he should. Maybe they should confront their past indiscretion once and for all, get it out of the way so they could forge on. Move forward. All that positive mumbo jumbo he'd never been much of a believer in.

"So what do you do? For exercise?" he finally asked, needing to get back on track and focus on Harper. Not become lost in old memories.

"I run mostly. A few mornings a week," she said with a little shrug. She set her slice of pizza on the plate and took a drink of her water. "I should probably run more, but…"

"Do you do anything else?"

"Sometimes Delilah gives a torturous exercise class during the summer. I've been known to participate in that." Harper made a little face. "She's kind of ruthless."

"This doesn't surprise me," he said, though he distinctly remembered Delilah complaining about her dance teacher and how relentless and pushy she used to be. Now Delilah was the relentless, pushy one.

"I should exercise more. I should do a lot of things that are good for me." She dropped her gaze to the table, a little sigh escaping her.

"Like what? And says who?" he asked.

Harper lifted her head, her pretty brown eyes meeting his. "This is going to sound incredibly lame," she started, her lips immediately clamping shut, as if she didn't want to say the rest.

"Out with it," West encouraged. "Come on, Harper. We're friends, right?"

Her gaze never strayed from his and after a few seconds of silence, he wanted to squirm in his chair like a little kid until she finally said, "Is that what we are, Weston? Friends?"

He froze. Here it was, their moment of truth. He could run right over this moment and not acknowledge their past or he could throw it out on the table and see how she reacted. What would she do if he told her he was attracted to her now? Still?

What would he do if she wasn't interested in him at all?

West frowned. He wasn't sure. And he didn't know if he wanted to consider either possibility yet.

"I thought maybe…" Her voice trailed off and she looked away, as if she couldn't face him. He got it. His heart pounded like a freight train, rattling his ribs as he waited for what she had to say next. "After what happened that last night you were in Wildwood, before you left. Things changed between us, Weston. They changed a lot."

She was right. Things had totally changed. But he never thought he'd have to see her again. He'd thought that he could just walk away from her and pretend that night had never happened.

But it had. And he suddenly, desperately wanted to talk about it. Own it. Reenact it.

Would she let him? Did she want him to?

Chapter Seven

Harper's heart was racing. If West agreed that yeah, they were nothing but friends and that night meant nothing to him, she would bolt, leave this place and never look back because she wouldn't be able to take his rejection again.

He took a deep breath, like he needed it for courage. "We've known each other for a long time," he started.

"And you've been gone for a long time," she finished. Did he see her as the same silly little Harper Hill? His little sister's best friend? God, she hoped not. She'd changed. So much so, she didn't feel like the same person anymore. Even the girl she was before, that night when she and West kissed, she wasn't her anymore either. She was older.

Supposedly wiser.

Maybe not so much, considering she was sitting there waiting with bated breath to hear what West had to say next.

"There are a lot of things I regret," he said, ducking his head so he stared at the table, pushing his plate away from him. "The last time we were together years ago, I didn't handle things between us right. And I'm—I'm sorry about that, Harper. So damn sorry."

He said nothing else and neither did she. She couldn't find the words, could hardly find any air left in her lungs. Was that all he had to say? Was he rejecting her again? God, she'd been right all along. She was supposed to protect her pride, protect her heart, and instead she'd laid it bare like a complete idiot.

Yet again.

Pushing away from the table, she stood, hurrying out of the tiny dining area without saying a word.

"Harper," she heard West call after her but she ignored him, too busy trying to get the hell out of there, too panicked he might try to say something else. Like how they should just be friends and there was nothing going on between them and what, she took that night of glorious kissing seriously? How silly could she be?

Yeah, she couldn't face that. No way.

Grabbing her purse from where she'd left it, she slung the strap over her shoulder and reached for the front door handle just as West crowded her from behind. He slapped his hand flat against the door, preventing her from escaping, surrounding her completely with his big, warm body.

She went completely still, the air stalling in her lungs as she tried to regain her composure. Surely she was overreacting. But he'd rattled her so completely it was hard for her to keep it together. Just being near him made her want to do stupid, reckless things.

Like throw herself at him. Beg him to kiss her again like he had so long ago. Feel his arms come around her and hold her close. She wanted all of that, as crazy as it sounded. She may have been with Roger, may have even thought that she wanted to marry him at one point, but the truth was right here, standing directly behind her, literally breathing down her neck.

She wasn't over West Gallagher. Not by a long shot.

"You didn't let me finish what I was going to say," he murmured, his fingers tangling in her hair, brushing it away from her neck. She sucked in a breath, tingles sweeping over her skin when he stepped even closer. Her purse slipped from her shoulder and she let it fall, heard it land on the tiled entryway with a soft clatter. "I don't want to push you to do anything you don't want, Harper. I know you just broke up with your boyfriend."

She trembled all over. He was so close he must've felt her body shaking. His fingers were still in her hair, skimming her nape, and she closed her eyes, overwhelmed by his simple touch.

"Ever since I saw you in the supermarket I haven't stopped thinking about you," he admitted, his voice low, so close it felt like he was speaking directly into her ear. "You looked so pretty, even when you were mad and insulting me."

Embarrassment threatened to swallow her whole. She *never* acted like that. There was something about West that brought out the worst in her.

Or maybe he brought out the real her.

"I remember exactly what you felt like in my arms, that night I kissed you," he continued. "What you tasted like. The sounds you made. How you'd clutch me closer every time I tried to pull away."

She dipped her head forward, her eyes tightly closed as she remembered too. The way he felt, the sounds he made, the way he tasted. He shifted closer, his mouth— oh, God, his *mouth*—was right at her nape, his hands resting lightly on her hips. "I'm curious to see if it's still just as good between us," he murmured against her skin, his warm lips making her shiver.

His hands on her body and his mouth moving against her neck made her want to melt. It was going to be good. So good she would probably combust at first touch of his mouth on hers.

"Turn around, Harper," he whispered into her hair, and she opened her eyes, turning slowly so she could face him. Her knees were so wobbly she leaned against the front door so she wouldn't fall to the ground in a boneless heap. West stepped into her personal space, his big hands braced against the door on either side of her head, his intense gaze zeroed in on her lips. "I didn't plan on this happening tonight."

"Plan on what happening tonight?" she asked with a slight frown. Oh, God, maybe he didn't want her after all. Maybe he was trying to let her down easy? She should've just left. It was complete torture, knowing he was most likely going to say something nice so he wouldn't hurt her feelings. She held her breath, waiting for the inevitable blow.

"This."

His lids lowered as he dipped his head, his mouth landing on hers, and her eyes slid closed once more, relief flooding her as she automatically reached for him, looping her arms around his neck. He didn't touch her, his hands remained on the door, but his mouth did wondrous things. Soft and seeking, warm and damp, his lips brushed against hers once. Twice. She parted her lips beneath his the third time, but he didn't take it any deeper. No, he was slow, methodical, purposeful. Learning her, driving her out of her mind.

He put some space between them and she slowly opened her eyes to find him watching her, his eyes glowing, his lips damp from her own. He was so close she could see the stubble lining his jaw, the faded scar just beneath his chin that he'd gotten when he crashed his bike into a fence at the age of eleven. It was kind of weird, kissing a man she'd known since he was a boy. Weird and...

Thrilling. Yes, definitely thrilling.

"Was it just as good as the last time we kissed?" she asked, surprised at her bravery. Pleased with her boldness. The simplest kiss in the world had the power to rattle her to the very depths of her soul. She sounded dramatic but it was true. West was exactly what she'd been searching for.

Passion.

"Better," he confessed with the faintest smile just before he kissed her again. He took it deeper this time, teasing just the inside of her mouth with slow sweeps of his tongue before circling it around her own. She clutched the soft hair at his nape, her fingers tugging, trying to pull him closer. He still hadn't put his hands on her and it was driving her crazy.

Harper tilted her chin up, her hair rubbing against the door as she tried to shift the kiss even deeper. But West wouldn't have it. He broke away from her, his mouth running along her jaw, down her throat, gently touching the sensitive spot just behind her ear. He bit her earlobe, making her gasp, her entire body throbbing with need.

And still he hadn't touched her.

"I know what you want," he whispered against her neck, sounding arrogant as hell. And so incredibly sexy too. If he knew what she wanted, then why wasn't he giving it to her? "But the second I put my hands on you it's all over."

"Wh-what's all over?" She bent her head to the left, giving him better access, and he took it, kissing and—*oh, God*—licking her neck.

Weston Gallagher had an amazing tongue.

"My self-control." He lifted his head, shifting himself away from her. "I'm afraid I'll tear your clothes off once I get my hands on you."

Her breath hitched in her throat at the thought. *Yes, please.* Oh, she'd never been lucky enough to have a man so overcome with need for her that he tore her clothes off. That sounded absolutely wonderful.

She slipped her hands away from his neck, over his shoulders, down his chest. He was firm. Muscular. And very, very warm. What would he do if she slipped her fingers beneath the hem of his T-shirt and lifted it right off him? Maybe *she* was tempted to lose all self-control and tear *his* clothes off.

Or maybe not. She was feeling brave tonight, but not that brave.

"Are you still mad at me?" he asked.

"I wasn't..." She shook her head.

West removed one hand from the wall, pressing his fingers against her lips and silencing her. "Don't lie to me, Harper. You were mad. That's why you were running out of here like your feet were on fire."

How did he know her so well? Maybe since she was so obvious? Probably. "I thought you were going to...let me down easy," she murmured against his fingers.

"I thought you were angry at me for attempting to make a move on you," he confessed, his hand dropping away from her mouth.

"Why would I be mad about that?" It was what she'd wanted for years.

"I come back into town, see you, and within twenty-four hours of our supermarket reunion, I hear you split with your live-in boyfriend. I figured you needed some time to...I don't know...heal? Not deal with some guy from your past acting like he wanted to get in your panties." He tucked a strand of hair behind her ear like he couldn't keep his hands off her.

Oh. Did he really want to get in her panties? The only words floating through her brain were *yes, please*. And then, *when can we make that happen?*

Whoops. That was definitely more than two words.

"You wanted to, um, get in my panties?" Her voice squeaked on the last word. She actually said *panties* to West. And they were in reference to *her* panties. She should be mortified, but she wasn't. No, more like aroused.

Very aroused.

"I've wanted to get in your panties for years," he admitted, his voice so low she almost couldn't hear him. "You turned sixteen, and I immediately wanted to jump you."

Say what? She sucked in a sharp breath, laughing as she lightly slapped him on the chest. "You did not."

He nodded. "I did too. You got all those pretty curves and the braces came off? Forget it. I was done for."

"You were a senior when I turned sixteen." He'd had his pick of girls. All three Gallagher boys had a reputation. With their good looks, easygoing attitudes, and natural athleticism, they were extremely popular. Smart. Friendly. Guys wanted to be their friends. Girls wanted to be their girlfriends. Everyone was naturally drawn to them, and West was the most charismatic of the bunch.

Well, he was to Harper.

"I know. And my sister's best friend." He shook his head. "And underage. Just…I thought we were a bad idea."

Wow. She'd always thought they'd be a great idea. She couldn't believe he'd been interested in her for so long.

"I'm thinking we might still be a bad idea," he said softly, his words causing dread to seep into her skin, reminding her that they were definitely not on the same page.

They weren't even in the same freaking book.

She stiffened and curled her hands into fists, pushing him away from her. He went stumbling back, the shock on his face obvious. How stupid could she be? Falling for his lines? Letting him *kiss* her again?

Clearly he made her stupid. Like, unbelievably stupid. And she wasn't a stupid person. Though when it came to men, maybe she was. She felt all over the place. From calm, stable Roger to sexy, outrageous West—what in the world was she doing?

SHIT, SHIT, *SHIT*. Why'd he have to go and say that? Harper was looking at him like she wanted to rip his head off when only moments ago she'd been in his arms, his mouth on her smooth, soft neck, savoring all those sweet little sighs she made. It was just as good between them as the last time they'd kissed. No surprise. But she was sweet and warm and giving and so incredibly responsive. She wanted more from him. She didn't have to say it, but he knew. And she deserved to be with a man who wanted to give her more.

He didn't think he could be that man.

Running a hand through his hair, he kept space between them, waiting for her to grab her purse off the floor and leave. He wouldn't blame her. Couldn't hold it against her if she made her escape. Not that he wanted her to leave, but…

If she stayed, he'd fuck her. She deserved more than that, a quick fuck. And that was all he was good for. All he could offer. *Permanency* wasn't a part of his vocabulary. Being with a girl, having a relationship? He'd never really experienced one beyond high school stuff and that didn't count. Once he graduated and started working for Cal Fire, he'd never had time for a steady girlfriend. Ever.

He was twenty-eight years old and had no idea how to make a relationship work. How pitiful was he?

"I didn't mean to hurt your feelings by saying that, Harper," he started, but she glared at him, making his lips clamp shut. Damn it, he needed to get this out. Reassure her that it wasn't her, but him. "It's just…you deserve someone better than me."

She made a face. "Give me a break. Are you serious?"

Great, here she went, calling him out on his shit. Not that he didn't deserve it. "I'm not what anyone would call boyfriend material." That sounded lame. He scratched the side of his head, uncomfortable with the way she studied him. Like he was a bug pinned on a board, wiggling and desperate to make his escape. "Plus, you just came out of a long relationship. You have to agree trying to dive back into another one probably isn't the smartest move."

Her mouth dropped open, her upper lip curled in the slightest sneer. "Awfully arrogant, aren't you? Assuming I'd want to call you my boyfriend after one measly kiss?"

He blinked, surprised at her tone. She didn't sound like the Harper he knew. Not even close. "Isn't that what you—"

Harper interrupted him with a very firm shake of her head. "No, West. I never said I wanted to be in a *relationship* with you. You haven't been home in almost eight years. I hardly know you—or should I say the you that you are now."

"So what are you saying? That you want to *hook up* with me?" He started to chuckle, the idea so unfathomable, he could hardly wrap his head around it. Harper Hill didn't hook up with anyone. He couldn't imagine getting her into his bed, fucking her brains out, and then never really talking to her again. One, she wouldn't stand for it. And two…

Well.

Maybe he *could* imagine getting her into his bed. And fucking her brains out. All night long. Enjoying every single minute of having her naked and beneath him, sweaty and clinging to him while she cried out his name as he pounded deep inside her. Okay, yeah, he could definitely imagine that. But could he see himself walking away from her afterward?

No. He cared about her too much—as a friend. And that was why friends with such a long, shared history couldn't hook up. Too much other stuff had the potential to come between them.

For one, his sister would probably kill him if he hurt Harper. Her grandma would kick him out of his condo for screwing around with her granddaughter. If his parents ever found out, they'd be horrified. The entire town would gossip about them. His brothers would think he was crazy.

This could never work. Ever.

"If you're going to just stand there and laugh, I definitely don't want to hook up with you. *Ever.*" She bent and grabbed her purse off the floor, slinging it over her shoulder almost violently as she turned her back to him. "Thanks for the pizza. Good night."

"Harper," he started, but it was too late. She slipped through the door and slammed it behind her, leaving a fragrant cloud of her scent surrounding him. A delicious mixture of her lotion, shampoo, and perfume. "Damn it," he muttered, pacing around the front entryway, growling with frustration when he heard her car start outside.

Not the way he wanted to end his evening with Harper. He'd fucked it up royally.

But what else was new?

Chapter Eight

SATURDAY NIGHT. HARPER desperately needed a break, a way to escape her thoughts. Bad enough she was working on such a tedious project at her grandma's restaurant. Cleaning out old filing cabinets was not exciting in the least. Worse? With nothing much to focus on, her mind was always filled with West. West smiling at her when they agreed on a paint color. West goading her into eating more pizza dipped in disgusting, delicious ranch. West telling her he couldn't stop thinking about kissing her.

West actually kissing her...only to ruin it by opening his big mouth and saying the stupidest stuff imaginable. She'd run out on him and hadn't looked back. He'd hadn't called her, texted her, nothing. It had been nothing but radio silence.

Granted, it had been only twenty-four hours since she saw him last, but still. It felt like longer. Much longer.

So when Delilah texted asking if she wanted to go out to dinner, Harper immediately said yes. She waited for her friend at the restaurant now, a tiny, trendy place with beautifully simple menus that elegantly described salads and sandwiches and served chilled glasses of wine. The sort of place that appealed to tourists, where locals rarely stopped in to eat, it was the perfect setting for Harper's much-needed escape.

Wren wasn't able to join them since she was sick with a raging case of horrific stomach flu. No one wanted to be near her, so she was holed up in her tiny one-bedroom cottage trying to recover. Harper felt terrible even thinking this, but she'd never been so grateful for someone getting sick. Without Wren there, she felt free to confess what happened between her and West last night. Yeah, it was risky telling Delilah, but Harper felt like she was going to burst if she didn't tell someone that she kissed West. That she was in lust with West and couldn't stop thinking about him. That she had a wicked plan forming in her brain that involved him and she needed someone to tell her if she was being crazy or not.

She was being crazy. She had to be. But for once in her life, she sort of didn't care. She wanted to run with it. Go against type and surprise everyone, especially herself.

Oh, and West. Definitely West.

"Sorry I'm late!" Delilah sat in the chair across from hers, a big smile on her face as she pushed her long, dark hair away from her shoulder. "I got held up by one of the moms. She wanted to complain about her daughter's lack of focus."

"And that's your fault how?" Harper asked, setting the menu down.

Delilah shook her head. "Who knows? They love to blame me for everything. The reason that girl can't focus is because she's a spoiled brat who gets to do what she wants whenever she wants it. I try to get her to listen to me in class, but forget it. She's too busy mouthing off or spacing out. Or giggling with her friends."

"I already ordered you a glass of wine." As if on cue, the waiter appeared, setting their glasses on the table in front of them. "Want to get an appetizer?"

"The goat cheese and apple one sounds great," Delilah murmured, her gaze glued to the menu.

The moment the waiter took off with their appetizer order, Delilah set her menu on the table, blowing out a harsh breath. "Oh my God, that was totally awkward."

Harper frowned. "What was?"

"Our waiter? I went on a date with him once." Delilah held a hand up in front of her and examined her fingernails.

"You did? What's his name? How was it?" How did Harper not know this?

"His name is David and it was…not great. Oh, he's a nice guy and we had an okay time, but he wasn't doing it for me. Not my type." Delilah flicked her thumb against her middle finger, her nails clicking together.

"Who is your type?" Harper braced herself. If she said someone like West, she would die. That would end her plan to tell Delilah about her issues with him.

"I've sort of been all over the place when it comes to dating, but I think I've finally figured him out." Delilah splayed her fingers, ticking off her dream man's qualities. "Tall, with a take-charge attitude. Quiet. Strong. Calm. Protective. Responsible. Good in bed."

They both laughed over the last one. "That's a given," Harper said in agreement.

Delilah grinned. "Kind. Handsome. Maybe even a little standoffish sometimes, though never mean. I've come to realize I have a thing for the still-waters-run-deep sort of guy."

Harper knew without a doubt her friend was describing Lane Gallagher. He was all of those things and more.

The waiter came back to their table and took their order, making conversation with Delilah and allowing Harper the opportunity to watch her squirm. She didn't squirm often. Delilah was always so confident, so at ease with talking to anyone. Talking with the waiter she had no interest in, she looked like she wanted to slide under the table.

"I thought he'd never leave," Delilah whispered the moment he was gone.

Harper grinned and took a sip of her wine.

Delilah's eyes narrowed as she studied Harper. "What's up with you? Don't tell me Roger's trying to get you back."

"I haven't even heard from Roger since I moved out." He'd mailed her last paycheck, but otherwise, there'd been no word from him. Maybe he was mad. Maybe he was already over her.

"Do you regret breaking up with him?"

"No." Harper shook her head. "It was the best thing for me to do. He wanted to settle down, but all I was doing was settling. It wasn't fair to him."

"So now you're a free woman, yet your grandma is your roommate and you're working at the BFD." Delilah shook her head. "Honey, you need some excitement in your life and quick."

Here was her chance to spill her guts about West. Taking a deep breath, she decided to go for it. "Actually, I have had a little excitement in my life lately."

"Found a love letter written to your grandma among the boxes of receipts?" Delilah raised a brow.

Harper stuck her tongue out at her, making Delilah laugh. "No. Something happened between me and... someone else." *Chicken. Can't even say his name out loud.*

Delilah leaned forward, her eyes dancing with excitement. "Ooh, don't hold back! Tell me who it is. And what exactly happened with you and this mysterious someone. I want all the dirty details."

Harper actually blushed. Damn her pale skin. "There are no real dirty details."

"Then why the blush?"

"You'll never believe who my someone is." Harper pressed her lips together, nerves eating at her insides. Maybe she shouldn't tell Delilah after all. She might flip out. She might try to convince her she was making a mistake—and maybe she was. She probably was. Okay fine, she *totally* was, but nothing could change her mind. The idea of letting West go filled her with panic. Yeah, he'd been a jerk last night, but he'd been honest.

And now she was contemplating taking him up on that honest offer and seeing where it might take them…

Okay. Maybe that wasn't the smartest choice, but it was definitely a selfish one. And since when had she ever been selfish when it came to being with a guy? She was a giver. She always had been. With Roger, she'd deferred to him on everything. Every choice, every matter, every meal, every TV show. It was all for Roger, never for her.

Well, she was done. Now she wanted to do something for herself. And she was considering doing…

West.

"Let me guess." Delilah's gaze never wavered from Harper's. "It's West."

Harper's jaw dropped open. "How did you know?"

The smug look on Delilah's face was obvious. "I saw the way he looked at you at the supermarket. I'd recognize that look anywhere."

Harper leaned back in her chair. "What do you mean?"

"He looked like he wanted to gobble you up. And in the best possible way too." Delilah smiled. "So, what happened between you two? Does Wren know about this?"

"No," Harper said quickly. "Wren doesn't have a clue and you can't tell her. She will flip the heck out." She proceeded to give Delilah all the details, right down to what West said before she left the condo.

"And I haven't heard from him since," Harper finished, shaking her head.

"It's only been a day," Delilah pointed out. "Oh, and he's an idiot. I just needed to state that for the record."

"He's a total idiot," Harper agreed. "But he's a sexy, sweet idiot and I think I want to go talk to him. He's off work tonight. Tomorrow night too." Imagine the many things they could be doing for the next two nights…

Okay, seriously. Did she really want to fool around with West? Have a no-holds-barred fling with him? One night together and then they could walk away. No attachments. No obligations.

She couldn't believe she was considering such an arrangement, but her life was already in complete upheaval so what the hell.

"What do you have in mind?"

"Well, that's where I think I need advice." Harper chewed on her lower lip. She'd never been as open about her sex life like Delilah and Wren were. "I need some more…excitement in my life."

"Of the sexual kind?"

Harper nodded. "And I want to see if West is up for the challenge."

"I'm sure he is."

"Maybe so, but maybe not with me?" Harper sighed. "All that talk about him feeling unworthy worries me. Like he'll never make a move on me because he thinks I'm long-term material when he's looking for a short-term girl."

"And you want to be his short-term girl?"

Harper nodded. She wasn't ready for any sort of commitment, no matter what West said. She wanted something fun. Hot. Mind blowing.

Passionate.

The secretive smile curling Delilah's lips made Harper smile in return. "Then I know just the thing for you to do to blow his socks off. Even if he's not wearing any socks."

They both started to laugh.

"I'm serious though. You'll need to be bold," Delilah said.

"I can do that." Harper nodded, excitement bubbling up inside her.

Excitement accompanied by a very fine case of nerves. Bold had never been her thing. She was a linger-in-the-background type of woman, always had been.

But when it came to West, he made her want to do something crazy. She just wasn't sure if he was interested in her type of crazy.

"Like, really bold. I'm talking about throwing it all out there. Letting him know exactly what you want from him so he won't misunderstand your intentions." Delilah watched her. "Once you start, you can't stop."

She smiled, pushing past her normal anxiety. "Trust me, I'm up for the challenge."

WEST WAS FUCKING exhausted. He'd spent most of the afternoon into the night painting the kitchen and dining area. The painting part wasn't exhausting though. It was all the prep. Taking down the pictures on the walls, taping off the baseboards and the ceilings, cleaning the walls, laying out the drop cloths to protect the floors. That shit took forever.

And he was over it.

He'd taken a shower and had only bothered to slip on a pair of basketball shorts. He was sprawled out on the couch, watching TV and nursing a beer. All alone on a Saturday night; how pathetic could he get?

Not much more pathetic.

Holden had called him, asking if he wanted to meet at a bar, but West turned him down. Lane had a day off too, but once they were done with Home Depot, he'd gone home and locked himself away in his tiny house, like he might melt if he got caught outside after sundown.

Not that West wanted to hang out with Lane. And he was too damn tired to keep up with Holden tonight. He'd rather stay home and watch shitty TV, nurse his emotional wounds, and hope like hell work would pick up soon so he could at least keep himself busy and not think about how he'd blown it with the girl of his secret dreams. It was late, past ten o'clock, and he should've just gone to bed but there was no point. He was wide awake, and he'd already jacked off in the shower so he would've just laid in bed and stared at the ceiling.

No thanks.

A knock sounded at his door, startling him, and he climbed off the couch to go answer it, pissed that it was most likely Holden ready to convince him he should go out to the bars. He didn't bother looking through the peephole, just unlocked the door and swung it open, launching right into a speech for his little brother.

"I already told you I didn't want to go out tonight," West said, the rest of the words stalling in his throat when he saw who was standing on his front doorstep.

It was Harper, wearing a black trench coat on a warm June night, her long auburn hair extra wavy and flowing past her shoulders, a secretive little smile curving her very red lips.

"You did?" She blinked up at him, all wide-eyed sexy innocence. "Maybe I should go then?"

She started to turn and he grabbed hold of her arm, halting her progress. "Don't go." He sounded eager. Way too eager. Clearing his throat, he started over. "Sorry. I just thought—I thought you were Holden."

"Oh." She turned to fully face him once more and his gaze dropped to her feet, which were in the sexiest, shiniest black high-heeled shoes he'd ever seen. "So you don't mind that I stopped by?"

He looked up, their eyes meeting. "Not at all." What was she up to? Her eyes were heavily made up, as were her ruby red lips. And her hair was downright wild…all he could think of was fisting it in his hands and tugging her head back so he could plant a long, deep kiss on those juicy lips.

"It's sort of late." She blatantly scanned his mostly naked body, her glossy lips parted, her pink tongue touching just the corner of her mouth. Her gaze lingered on his chest and arms, cataloging his tattoos. She seemed fascinated with them and he was half tempted to flex his muscles just to see if her eyes grew hungrier…

Which they seemed to do, without any encouragement on his part. If she didn't stop looking at him like that he might get a freaking boner and that probably wouldn't be good. "Were you in…bed?"

The provocative way she just said it made him aware of her close proximity. How her hands tugged on the ends of the belt wrapped tight around her waist. The hollow of her throat was exposed, as was a bit of her chest. She looked practically naked under that coat.

Hmm.

"No, I wasn't in bed." He paused, wondering what the hell she was up to. Whatever it was, he could appreciate the way she was staring at him, and he was damn thankful she'd come by. He figured he'd blown it for good with Harper. "You want to come in?"

"I would love to." She smiled and he stepped out of her way, the scent of her surrounding him as she walked by. He shut and locked the door and followed her as she moved deeper into the living room. Grabbing the remote from the side table, he turned off the TV, the sudden silence amplifying every move she made.

"So I have a proposition for you," she said, turning to face him once more. "One I'm hoping you'll agree to."

In the hushed quiet of his house, she looked a little less sure, a little more nervous. A lot more like the Harper he knew. He wanted to reach out and reassure her, but he also wanted to hear what she had to say first.

"Really?" He rested his hands on his hips, noting the way her gaze dropped to linger on his stomach. He felt downright exposed, what with the way she studied him. Not that he minded. "What is it?"

She bit her lower lip as she contemplated him, her straight white teeth a bold contrast to the deep red coating her lips. "Last night, when we talked, you said you weren't boyfriend material."

He winced. Did he really need a reminder of the stupid things he'd said?

"And I told you I wasn't looking for a relationship, which is true. I don't want one. But I do want *something* from you, West." She reached for the coat belt, slowly undoing it. "I'm hoping you want the same thing."

Oh, shit. He was fairly certain he knew what was about to happen. She'd shed the coat and—he hoped— she would be wearing nothing much underneath. And if she was asking for uncomplicated sex, could he give her that? Did he want to give her that?

She bent her head and undid the belt, letting it fall to the floor. Glancing up at him, she didn't smile, didn't say anything. Just held his gaze while her fingers moved over the few buttons keeping the coat together, until the last button was undone and the coat fell open. Revealing that she wore nothing but the smallest scrap of black lacy panties he'd ever had the honor of seeing.

He broke out into an immediate sweat. Yeah. He'd give her whatever she wanted, no questions asked.

"Sit down, West," she demanded and he did, practically falling backward onto the couch, his hands gripping his knees. He told himself to calm the hell down, but the quick mental reassurance was no help. He had an erection just from seeing her like this, watching her move toward him with pure determination in her every step as she shrugged out of the coat so it fell onto the floor in a crumpled heap.

She pushed his hands away from his knees and strad-dled his thighs, her bare breasts in his face, hard, rosy pink nipples a complete temptation. Ignoring them, he tilted his head back, blinking up at her as she smiled down at him, shaking her head so her hair tumbled all to one side.

"Like what you see?" she asked, her voice husky. Sexy.

So unbelievably sexy he couldn't believe this was hap-pening. How'd he get so fucking lucky?

"I definitely like what I see," he said, his gaze…every-where. He didn't know what to look at first. Her face? Her breasts? Those slender legs straddling him, the lace pant-ies and what lay beneath? Christ, she was trying to kill him. Slay him dead.

It was working.

Harper rested her hands on his shoulders, her fin-gers tracing the artwork that covered his skin. She drew closer, her hair trailing over his bare skin, and bent her head so her mouth was by his ear. "You should touch me, West. Touch me wherever you want."

Ah, fuck. Closing his eyes, he pressed his lips together when she kissed his neck, her hot, damp lips driving him insane. Her hands slid down his chest, her hips shifted forward, and he swallowed hard, desperate to keep his shit together.

He settled his unsteady hands on her hips, slipping his fingers underneath the thin lace. She went still beneath his palms, her warm breath fluttering against his neck. Spreading his fingers wide, he slid them over her soft, plump ass, pulling her in closer. So she could feel exactly what she was doing to him.

"Despite your worry last night, I can handle uncomplicated. I can be whatever you want me to be," she whispered against his throat, her lips tickling his skin.

Yeah. This was probably a huge mistake. But he was beyond the point of thinking or worrying about mistakes. His control was this close to snapping completely. Her hair was in his face, her mouth on his neck, her ass in his hands. She surrounded him, soft fragrant scent and panting breaths and trembling skin. They were both close enough to naked that it didn't take much imagination to figure out what it would feel like, to have Harper bare and in his arms.

"You feel so good," she whispered as she lifted up so she hovered above him, her hands settling on his cheeks. He tilted his head back as she moved in, her mouth landing on his as she kissed him. Devoured him.

He let her take control, content in the taste of her, the feel of her. Where had this bold version of Harper come from? He wasn't complaining. This was the push he needed. For whatever reason, this woman made him nervous. Hesitant. Unsure. He kept blaming it on their past, on their friendship, but maybe it was something more.

Maybe it was because he cared about her too damn much. He didn't want to hurt her. Didn't want to ruin their friendship. For once in his damn life, he wasn't being completely selfish when it came to sex. He worried about her.

West wanted to make her happy. Leave her satisfied. Any other woman, he would've taken over by now. Taken command of the kiss, of the entire situation. Hell, he'd probably be inside her already, or at least with a condom in hand and his intent clear.

But now, in this moment with Harper, he wanted to savor her. Let her draw it out and get what she wanted from him before he took over and demanded what he needed from her.

Her tongue tangled with his, her hands clutching his face, the little whimpering sounds in the back of her throat making him want to pull her hair and kiss her deeper. But he didn't. He kept his hands on her ass, fingers tugging and pulling at the flimsy fabric of her panties, brushing against her sensitive, rarely touched skin. She shivered beneath his hands, breaking the kiss so she could take a breath, and he stared up at her, watching as she took deep breaths, the way her breasts moved, her nipples like hard little points, beckoning him.

Giving in to the urge, he leaned forward and licked one, making her gasp. Drew it into his mouth and sucked, making her moan. She tasted sweet. Her lower body squirmed against his, driving him out of his fucking mind, and he went still. Tried to count to five and get his bearings, get his shit under control.

But it was no use. She pushed and pushed, what with the way she writhed against him, her delicious nipples and sexy sounds. He shredded her panties, tearing them from her body so they clung to his hands, little bits of ruined black lace. He dropped them to the floor and gripped her hips, his fingers pressing into her skin. He could smell her arousal, knew that she was wet, wet for *him*, and that was fucking it.

His control snapped, leaving him completely.

Chapter Nine

HARPER'S PANTIES WERE gone. Torn to shreds by West's hands, all while he sucked and licked her nipples. Talk about hot. She'd never had a man do something like that to her before.

It was…

Awesome.

The way he'd watched her so hungrily when she got rid of the coat, when she sat on top of him and told him to touch her…she'd never felt so powerful before. And he'd done everything she'd asked, even more than what she asked for.

But the power had switched and he'd taken over. Somehow, she ended up on her back on the couch, West's hips between her legs, his mouth on her chest as he rained kisses all over her skin. She buried her hands in his thick hair, clutching him close, moaning when he licked and sucked her nipples, her legs wrapping around his hips.

She could feel his erection nestled firmly between her legs and um, wow. He was huge. They were probably moving too fast. Way too fast. But she didn't care. She wanted West, any way she could get him.

"Christ you taste good," he murmured against her chest. He shifted downward, his mouth running across her stomach, drawing closer and closer to that throbbing spot between her legs. She didn't think she was ready for that and she tugged on his hair, trying to bring him up to her mouth so she could kiss him.

He got the hint and moved so they were face-to-face, lips to lips. He kissed her, his hand sliding down her belly, settling between her legs. She gasped at his first brazen touch, the way his assured fingers slipped between her folds, searching. Teasing, Finding her clit, circling it, his mouth locked with hers, his tongue sweeping.

She was close already. Embarrassingly close. It was like he understood her body, knew exactly what she needed to get off. The few men she'd been with had needed an instructional manual and a map and they still hadn't been that great at finding the necessary parts to ensure she'd experience an orgasm. Her coming was usually such an afterthought that she'd become quite the expert at taking care of herself.

"Oh, God." She tore her mouth from his, needing to catch her breath and concentrate on the feel of his fingers moving between her thighs. She sucked in a breath, and her lips parted as she felt the familiar tug and pull low in her belly. This was all happening so fast. When she'd put the plan together with Delilah earlier, she wasn't sure how West would respond.

Worse, she'd wondered if she could even go through with it.

Thank goodness she'd dug up some of that buried courage. Look at her now.

"You gonna come, Harper?" His voice was pure intent. Pure sex. A shudder moved through her and he whispered again, his mouth against her cheek. "I want to make you come, baby. Are you close?"

She nodded, too overcome to speak.

"Tell me where to touch you to make you fall apart." His voice went even deeper, if that was possible. He slid one finger inside her body, and she stiffened, sucking in a breath. "You like that?"

"Yesss." She lifted her hips, bit her lip when he sunk another finger inside her body. "More," she whimpered. "Faster."

"That's my girl." He increased his pace, thrusting his fingers inside her welcoming body, drawing her closer and closer to that delicious edge. She liked what he said to her, how he encouraged her to ask for what she wanted. And she wanted to ask for more, beg for it, but she was still feeling a little shy.

Which was absolutely ridiculous, considering she was completely naked and his fingers were between her legs while he was urging her to come.

He removed his hand and her eyes flashed open, watching as he brought his fingers to his mouth and sucked them. "You taste fucking unbelievable," he murmured and she was filled with the desperate urge to shove his face between her legs so she could feel his tongue lick her there. *Oh, God, that would feel amazing.* Forget being shy. Forget worrying over what he might see down there.

She wanted him to lick her straight to oblivion.

"West." She felt restless. Needy. Her voice was soft. Thin. He looked at her like he knew exactly what she wanted.

Dropping a quick kiss on her lips, he smiled at her. "You want me to go down on you?"

Her cheeks were warm. Her entire body was hot. She nodded and he kissed her again, his tongue pushing inside her mouth for a too-quick moment.

Then he moved down. Farther. Farther...

Until his hands were spreading her thighs wide and he ran his tongue over her sex, licking her everywhere. She arched into his mouth, a shaky moan escaping her when he added two fingers, pushing them deep inside her. She was so close. So incredibly close to coming and she strained beneath his ministrations, her entire body shaking as she sought her release.

"Relax," he murmured against her, his hands sliding beneath her butt and holding her close. "Just let it happen, baby."

She closed her eyes and did exactly what he requested. She slowly went lax, concentrating on the feel of him, his fingers curling inside her body as he circled her clit with his tongue. Reaching out, she touched his hair, speared her fingers through the silky softness, felt him whisper against her flesh. God, she was wet, so wet, but he didn't seem to care. No, he seemed to like it. He sucked her clit between his lips, thrusting his fingers faster and she was done for.

A cry fell from her lips as she shattered completely. Her entire body shook with orgasm and he never let up, his mouth still working her sex, his fingers still moving inside her body. She clutched at his hair, arched into his face and still he kept on, until finally she had to practically push him away to make him stop.

"Sorry," she said after he rose up to pull her into his arms. "I was a little sensitive."

He kissed her forehead. "That was fucking hot," was all he said. He slipped his fingers beneath her chin, tilted her face up, and kissed her.

She didn't flinch at the taste of herself on his lips. He opened his mouth wide, the kiss turning carnal. Sloppy. They rolled around as best they could on the narrow couch until finally he broke the kiss first, whispering against her lips, "Do you have a condom?"

"In my trench coat pocket," she whispered back, surprised that he didn't have any.

He slid off the couch and went to the trench coat that lay crumpled on the floor, pulling the handful of condoms she'd shoved into her pocket before she left her house. Condoms that Delilah had dumped into her purse at her house, where Harper had borrowed the heels and the trench.

Heels that she'd kicked off at some point during this incredibly amazing interlude with West. Appearing at his front door wearing nothing but a pair of panties beneath a borrowed coat was definitely well-thought-out encouragement.

And now they were going to take it one step further. Anticipation made butterflies flutter madly in her stomach and she bit her lower lip, pushing her hair out of her face as she watched him stride toward her, still wearing the basketball shorts, his erection creating a very aggressive tent in the front of them.

"Brought enough?" he asked, flashing the three condom wrappers at her with a smile. He deposited two of them on the side table, his hands going to the waistband of his shorts. She sat up quickly, batting his hands away.

"Let me," she murmured, her mouth literally watering at seeing him naked for the first time.

He stood in front of her, completely still as she curled her fingers into the waistband of his shorts, her knuckles brushing against his bare skin and making him shiver. She tipped her head back, staring up at him, and she hoped she looked sexy and not a complete mess. He was beyond sexy—fierce and gorgeous, with the tattoos covering his upper body, making her curious. Why those particular tattoos? And why so many? She knew he'd always been a bit of a rebel growing up, but now he just looked like a badass.

A badass she was about to strip completely naked.

Her heart still beat erratically, making her breath come rapidly, and she tore her gaze from his at the same time she pulled his shorts down. Past his hips, past his very thick cock, until they fell to his feet and he kicked them off, his erection bobbing with the movement.

Licking her lips, she touched his hard thigh, running her fingers up until she curled them around the base of his cock. He groaned, his hand going to the side of her head, fingers sliding into her hair. She dropped a kiss to the very tip of him, marveling at the arousal she felt coursing through her veins, at how quickly she became wet again between her legs. Blowjobs were usually something she did as an obligation, an act she performed in hopes of a returned favor.

And it was something she always had to work up to. Going down on someone was so intimate, at least it was to her. But maybe it helped that she'd known West for so long. She trusted him.

That was huge.

Harper wrapped her lips around the very tip of his erection, tasting him. Licking the head, drawing her tongue down the length of him, then back up.

"You suck my cock between your lips and I'll blow," he said from between gritted teeth. "It'll all be over."

She pulled away from him slightly and smiled, flicking her hair over her shoulder as she stared up at him. "That's okay. Maybe you could come all over my chest?" Oh, that sounded amazing. No one had ever done that to her before. She always thought it was too dirty, even sometimes too degrading an act for her to actually you know…want.

But she did want it. With West. From the look on his face, he wanted it too.

"Jesus, Harper." He squeezed his eyes shut, the muscles in his neck and jaw strained. Taking a deep, fortifying breath, he slowly opened his eyes, their blue depths glowing with unbridled arousal. "We'll do that later, okay? I promise. Right now, I need to be inside you."

He gave her no chance to argue. Just took right over, pressing her against the couch, fumbling with the condom as he tore the wrapper from it. He rolled the ring of rubber onto the head of his cock, sheathing himself, and she watched in fascination, thankful they'd left the lights on. West's body was a thing of masculine beauty and when he drew closer, she ran her hands over his chest, tracing her fingers through the dark hair between his pecs, along the tattoos that covered his skin. He was hot and hard and leanly muscular. Strong and capable and sexy. She felt like she just hit the sex lottery.

And they'd only just gotten started.

HARPER MADE HIM a nervous, fumbling mess. Just watching her kiss and lick his dick had almost sent him straight over the edge. West knew if she would've sucked him into that sweet mouth of hers, he would've blown his wad in seconds. He had to stop her, no matter how much he regretted it.

And when she'd mentioned him coming on her tits? Fucking forget it. It was all he could see, all he could *still* see. Fisting his cock, his semen splattering all over her smooth skin, dripping off her nipples. The filthiest scene he could imagine and it was with Harper. Sweet little Harper Hill. Fuck.

Just…fuck.

He almost screwed up getting the condom on too. Being with Harper made him feel young. Eager. Capable of doing anything, saying anything, being whatever she wanted. She watched him closely, with adoration in her eyes, like he could solve world peace and make her come, all in one swoop. He felt like he could do that too. Being in Harper's arms, kissing her, his face in her pussy, whatever, wherever…when he was with her, he felt like he could conquer the damn world.

And that was heady stuff.

"How do you like it?" he asked, causing her head to jerk up, her startled gaze meeting his. "You want me on top or you on top?"

She contemplated his questions, her teeth sinking into her swollen lower lip. Her lipstick had faded, leaving behind a faint red smudge, and it made her look even sexier, if that was possible.

He had a distinct feeling that her past sexual partners hadn't discussed logistics much. Harper seemed to enjoy considering what she wanted to do with him. To him. He liked giving her the option as well.

This first time around, at least. Next time, it was all on him. He would choose what they were going to do.

And she would fucking love every minute of it.

"I want to be on top," she finally said, her voice soft, her eyes glowing. He grabbed her around the waist and pulled her on top of him, so he was sitting and she straddled him once again, his cock rising up between them, eager to get this party started. "Oh, I've never done it like this before," she admitted.

West frowned. Really? Then who the hell was this woman screwing, because they needed to get a freaking imagination.

Or maybe they didn't. He could show her how to do this. How to have fun. How to experiment. How to get as dirty and crazy as they wanted to be since it really didn't matter because they were doing it together.

"You're going to like it," he said as he rested his hands on her hips. "With you on top, I'll go extra deep."

Her gaze flared with heat at his words. She liked it when he talked, too, and he was holding himself back, not even letting the dirty words fly like he usually did.

He pulled her on top of him, grasping the base of his dick with one hand and guiding toward her entry. He pushed inside her hot, wet depths, both hands gripping her hips once more, and she slung her head back, her eyes sliding closed as she sank all the way down the length of his cock. Until he was fully embedded, throbbing deep inside her.

"*Oh.*" She kept her head thrown back, her tongue coming out to lick her lips, and he watched her in complete silent fascination. Her body bowed forward, her chest thrust toward him, pretty pink nipples begging for a lick, a suck. He released a shaky breath, trying to keep it together, but it was damn hard.

She was so beautiful, so sexy and so fucking real. He'd put this moment off for days. Hell, for years. That one amazing night when they'd kissed all those years ago, he'd known it would be good between them. That they would just naturally fit. From the first moment he saw her after arriving back in Wildwood, he'd had the same feeling again. It would be so good between them. The attraction was there. The spark, the heat, the trust, the friendship they shared burned brighter than ever.

He'd been putting off the inevitable. And now that he was inside her, that they were as connected as two human beings could be, he could kick himself for not doing this sooner.

Like eight years earlier.

"You were right," she said as her hips slowly started to move. She tipped her head toward his, her lips curled in a tiny smile. "You're so deep."

"You've really never been on top before?" Why the hell did he ask that? He didn't want to think of her with someone else, some other guy's dick inside her body. That was all sorts of fucked up.

"Well, I have." She made an awkward face, her lips quirking to the side. "But never like this."

"Mmm-hmm." He tightened his hold on her hips, his gaze locked on where their bodies were connected. His cock disappeared inside her body, in, out. In. Out. Christ, that was hot. He was sweating. The tingling had already started at the base of his spine and his balls drew up close to his body.

Damn it, he was going to come, and he wasn't ready yet.

"You feel so good." She started to increase her pace, lifting her arms up so she gathered her hair in her hands, piling it on top of her head. "I think I could come again."

Ah. That gave him reason to stop thinking about his orgasm barreling down on him. "You could?"

"Hmm." She was so lost in her own pleasure she didn't notice when he leaned in and drew her nipple into his mouth, sucking it lightly. A gasp escaped her and she curled her arms around his head, her hands in his hair as she mashed his face to her chest. "I really love it when you do that."

West had a feeling she loved it when he did anything to her.

Her leisurely pace soon became inadequate. He needed more. He needed faster, deeper penetration. Grabbing hold of her, he wrapped his arms around her body and held her still, lifting his hips so he could ram up inside her. A shocked moan left her lips and he clutched the back of her head, kissing her deep, thrusting his tongue inside her mouth in time with the thrusts of his cock inside her body.

She broke the kiss first, her breathing ragged, her damp body clinging to his. "S-so close," she whispered brokenly, her words only spurring him on.

He thrust deep. Deeper. His orgasm growing bigger, hovering closer, until finally he came with a shout and his entire body shuddered with the impact. Harper cried out, her arms wrapped tight around his neck, her face buried against his shoulder as she shivered uncontrollably. She clung to him and he clung to her, like they needed the closeness.

Savoring it.

Once he recovered, he smoothed his hand down her back, trying to calm her, calm himself. His heart racing, he took deep, even breaths, letting the hazy sleepiness that always seemed to come after an excellent bout of sex slowly wash over him.

Harper didn't allow them to wallow for long. She gently withdrew her body from his and, smiling down at him, dropped a kiss on his forehead before she took off for the bathroom without a word. Frowning, West watched her go, his gaze lingering on the pert curve of her ass.

Shit. Wasn't he supposed to be the one who went to the bathroom to take care of the condom? He pulled it off and got up, tossing it in the trash in the kitchen before making a mental note to throw that garbage outside first thing tomorrow morning. With his luck, one of his brothers would stop by and see a discarded condom in the trash and ask him whom he'd boned. They were that crude. And that nosy. Then again, so was he. Hell, he knew Lane would figure it out quick if he found even the smallest clue.

He was exiting the kitchen when Harper walked past him, headed straight for the trench coat, which she snatched off the floor and slipped back on her body, tying the fabric belt extra tight around her waist.

"Guess the panties are a lost cause." She nodded toward the discarded scraps of black lace scattered on the floor.

"Sorry about that." West rubbed his jaw, feeling like shit for destroying her panties. He didn't know what had come over him.

Harper. That's what came over you.

"Don't apologize. It was hot, the way you ripped them off my body. Like you couldn't control yourself." She smiled at him as she slipped on her impossibly high heels, wobbling a little bit. Reaching up, she finger combed her sexy-messy hair, glancing about the room like she might've forgot something else. As if she were looking for her opportunity to make her escape.

It suddenly dawned on him what she was doing.

"Are you leaving?" he asked incredulously.

"Well, yeah." She approached him, fully clothed. He felt a little raw—a lot on display since he was still completely naked—and he sort of hated how quick she was jetting out of there.

That was usually his job. He was the one who fucked and ran. Always.

"You sure you don't want to stay a little longer?" Damn it, he sounded pitiful. Clearly she didn't want to stay. She was already dressed and mentally on her way out.

"I really shouldn't, though thanks for the offer." She rested her hands on his chest and kissed him lightly. "I have to work tomorrow so I need a good night's sleep."

He slipped his arms around her waist, wishing she didn't have that stupid coat on. "You don't think you'd get a good night's sleep with me?"

"I know I wouldn't." She patted his chest and withdrew from his arms. "That was amazing," she whispered, kissing him one last time. "Thank you."

And with those last words, she slipped out of the house, closing the door quietly behind her.

West flopped back on the couch, running both hands through his hair.

What the hell just happened?

Chapter Ten

"I WANT DETAILS."

Harper shook her head, concentrating on dumping creamer in her coffee. It was early and the restaurant was quiet for a Saturday, thank goodness. She and Delilah had agreed to meet at a breakfast house normally frequented by tourists. Last thing she wanted was to run into someone one of them knew. "No way. I don't kiss and tell."

The only reason they were meeting was because Delilah had hoped Harper would kiss and tell—and tell and tell and tell some more.

"Come on. You gotta give me something." Delilah sounded completely put out. "Do you realize that West and I never actually did it?"

Harper paused in her stirring, surprise rendering her completely still. "Seriously?"

Delilah nodded. "I never even got to see what he was packing. We were young and stupid and scared. My mom drilled the fear of pregnancy into me. No way was I going to have sex, especially when I was only sixteen. I was terrified West would knock me up."

"Oh. Wow." Harper was stunned by Delilah's revelation. "Well, let's just say he knew exactly what he was doing."

And then some. West had seemed completely in tune with her body. She'd loved every minute of it. He'd given her not just one, but *two* orgasms, which was unheard of for her. Most of the time she didn't even have one during sex. Granted, the second one hadn't been a big one, but it had been pleasant. Especially with West buried deep inside her body, shouting his pleasure when his own orgasm swept over him.

Her body went warm at the memory.

"And did you rock his world?" Delilah smiled mischievously.

Harper grinned in return. "Yes. I definitely surprised him when I showed up at his front door. It was such a great idea for me to wear the trench coat. Thank you again." The look on his face when she'd taken it off had been worth the nerves shaking her to her very core.

She'd almost chickened out twice, making a U-turn and heading straight for home. She'd also sat in her car in the condominium parking lot, searching for courage before finally forcing herself to walk to West's front door. To think of all she would've missed out on if she had bailed…

"So now what?" Delilah prodded. Forget food, she wanted dirty details. But Harper needed a fortifying meal so she could work in her grandma's office for the rest of the day.

"What are you referring to?"

"What's going to happen next with you and West?"

Harper shrugged. "I don't know." She truly didn't. And she didn't want to think about it either. She'd rather take it day by day. It was easier that way. Without expectations, there was no need for worry. She wouldn't be disappointed. She'd just…be.

She was learning that when dealing with West, she needed to have no expectations at all. He didn't want serious, she knew this. It was best to keep it easy. No pressure. West bailed at the first sign of pressure.

At least, she thought he did. She still didn't understand why he'd never contacted her again after that one night they kissed. He'd left for a job, but that didn't mean he should've ditched her completely…

"Are you going to see him again? Did you two make plans?"

"No." A waitress approached, topping off their coffee cups, and they didn't speak until she left them alone. "What's the point? I figured we'll see each other again eventually."

"So you really are treating this whole thing as a casual affair?" Delilah sounded surprised.

"Well, yeah. There's no point in wanting more from West." She meant that, really she did. Yet, if he tried to turn what they had into something more serious, she'd be inclined to give it a go.

Oh, whom was she trying to kid? She'd totally go for it. She had feelings for West. But she was also trying to tell herself that she could settle for a purely sexual relationship with him. If she got in too deep, she'd walk.

Simple as that.

Hopefully.

"Listen, this isn't good enough." Delilah slapped the edge of the table, startling Harper so she jumped in her seat. "I need more details. You don't have to get graphic, but was he an attentive lover? He was a good kisser back in the day, so I can only imagine he's improved. Was he considerate? Dirty talker? Quiet grunts? Did he make sure you had an orgasm?"

"All of your questions require fairly graphic answers," Harper pointed out primly. "So…no comment."

"Come on, Harper, throw a dog a bone." Delilah lowered her voice. "Do you know how long it's been since I've had sex? I've gone through the most serious dry spell of my adult life. I'm dying over here."

"Don't you think it's weird that you're encouraging me to give you sex details about my encounter with your ex-boyfriend?" Harper thought it was pretty weird.

"No, that's the joy of living in a small town your entire life. Eventually we're going to have that six-degrees-of-separation thing," Delilah said with a nonchalant wave of her hand.

"More like two degrees," Harper muttered as the waitress approached again, a local newspaper folded in her hands.

"You gals want to look this over? The people that just vacated left it behind." When they both nodded the waitress dropped the paper in the middle of the table, startling them both. "Your breakfast is almost up," she said before she walked away.

They each grabbed for a section, Harper grabbing the front part. Yeah, most city newspapers were a dying art, but the *Wildwood Guardian* was still a staple among the townspeople. They loved their news and local gossip.

"My favorite section is the Daily Blotter," Delilah said as she flipped through the paper to find it. "Ah, here we go. *Monday, 2:22 a.m., Phyllis Corneal at 1147 Woodland Drive reported a break-in. Turned out it was the neighborhood bandit raccoons digging through her trash cans yet again.*" Delilah glanced up, a smirk on her face. "Direct quote."

The Daily Blotter was a full list of police and medical calls. They were mostly ridiculous. It was everyone's favorite section.

Harper scanned the front page, her gaze snagging on a headline.

Possible Arsonist in the Wildwood Lake Area.

Frowning, she read the article, but it didn't say much. Just talk of a few miscellaneous fires, a quote from Lane, along with one from Tate. Neither were encouraging talk of an arsonist, but they weren't denying the possibility either.

West had never mentioned an arsonist to her, though it wasn't like they'd talked much last night.

Again her cheeks went warm at the memory of exactly what they'd done. No way could she give Delilah details. How he kissed like a dream. How amazing his hands were as they roamed all over her body. The way he'd torn off her panties and shredded them into bits. How he made her come with his magical mouth and the ridiculous things she said to him and the sexy things he said to her…

"Oh, crap. They're here," Delilah whisper-hissed from across the table. She held her newspaper up in front of her face, rattling the paper so it made an annoying crinkling noise. "Put your paper up!"

Harper did as she commanded, holding the front section of the *Guardian* up so it covered her entire head. "Who's here? Who are we hiding from?"

"Freaking Lane and Weston! What are they doing here? Only tourists come to this dump." Delilah sounded about as panicked as Harper felt. "God, he's wearing his uniform too."

Harper swore she heard Delilah whimper.

Taking a deep breath, she told herself to focus. So West was here. So what? He was allowed to go out to breakfast the day after they'd had the most amazing sex of her life. She'd known she'd run into him eventually, she just hadn't thought the moment would come so soon.

Carefully, she peeked around the edge of the newspaper, watching as the waitress escorted them to their table. She was young, her smile was big, and her chest was thrust out, as if she was desperately showing off her boobs. Lane was in his uniform, looking like he was about to go on duty, and he flashed the woman a polite smile but otherwise didn't pay her any mind. West didn't either. He seemed distracted. The relief that Harper felt at seeing this shouldn't have made her so happy.

But it did.

"Tell me they're clear across the room from us," Delilah said.

"They're clear across the room from us," Harper lied. They were really only about halfway across the room—and in their direct line of vision.

Meaning, the moment they set down the newspapers, they'd be caught.

Delilah checked around her newspaper, then sent her a glare. "You lied. They're not clear across the room."

"You asked me to tell you that." Harper paused. "You didn't ask if it was true."

"Dude, you're feisty after you get some. Jeez." With a sigh, Delilah set the paper down, putting herself on display. "May as well get it over with," she muttered under her breath.

Now that she'd been hiding behind the newspaper shield, Harper felt kind of stupid lowering it. Would it be obvious that she was hiding from West? If it weren't for Delilah commanding for her to do so, she would've never hid. She would've smiled and waved at him and then carried on her conversation with Delilah. Killed him with nonchalance. She knew it would've driven him insane.

One bit of advice Delilah had given her that had stuck was pretending she didn't care. No matter how much it killed her, she needed to keep up the pretense that what she and West had shared was casual. Though really...was it much of a pretense? She sort of liked this newfound freedom. The idea that she could have no-strings-attached sex with a hot guy—a hot guy she'd actually crushed on when she was younger—had always been inconceivable.

But why? The only person who was holding her back was…

Her.

Deciding to hell with it, she dropped the newspaper and folded it, throwing it at Delilah, who batted it away with an annoyed laugh. Of course, the sound drew the Gallagher men's attention and their heads both swiveled in their table's direction.

West smiled, his gaze warm and intimate. As if communicating just with his eyes their shared moments from last night. She smiled back, her gaze skipping right over him and landing on Lane, who was staring at Delilah like he was a starving dog and she was a very juicy, delectable bone.

Harper looked at Delilah, but she wasn't paying Lane any mind. Too busy resuming her Daily Blotter reading, the idiot woman. Why were her two closest friends lusting over guys who lusted over them too, yet none of them seemed to make a move? It made no sense.

She was the quiet one. The meek one who was never expected to make any sort of move. Yet she'd gone after West like she was the ballsiest one of them all. It was kind of crazy.

Her gaze returned to West, who was rising from his chair, his eyes still on her. Her heart started to beat faster as he made his way to their table, his stride slow and easy, his smile downright hungry.

An answering hunger rose deep within her, her skin tingling as he drew closer. He looked good, wearing a pair of jeans and a gray T-shirt, his hair a little damp like he just got out of the shower.

Hmm. She wondered if he'd be interested in taking a shower with her sometime. That could be hot. She'd never tried shower sex before.

"Morning, ladies." West stopped directly in front of their table, though he looked only at Harper. "Surprised to see you two here."

"More like you should be worried," Delilah said to him. "Harper is spilling all of your secrets to me, West."

The look of pure, unadulterated panic that swept over his face would've made Harper laugh in any other situation, but not this one. Nope, she was pissed at her friend and gave her a good kick under the table to shut her up.

"Ow, *shit*," Delilah whispered, glaring at her.

Harper glared right back before sending West a serene smile. "She's just pulling your leg. I promise."

He still looked nervous. Edgy. "Well. Good to know." His chuckle was forced. "I'll let you two get back to your breakfast. Just wanted to say hi."

Harper watched him go, longing filling her the farther away he got. She'd been half tempted to invite him to join her. Just so she could sit next to him. Hear him talk. Watch him smile. Listen to him breathe.

Great, now she sounded like a freaking stalker. Frowning, she tore her gaze away from his retreating form.

"He came over here to talk to you," Delilah whispered.

She turned on her friend, glaring at her once more. "Until you blew it."

Delilah winced. "Sorry. I couldn't help it. My big mouth gets me in trouble all the time, I swear."

"Now he thinks I was telling you his dick size." Harper watched as he slid back into his chair and spoke to Lane, before they glanced in her direction. The both of them looked away hurriedly when she caught them.

That couldn't be good.

"I mean, I have an estimate in my head, but you can be more specific if you'd like," Delilah offered so graciously.

"Seriously, Dee. I'm going to run over there and tell Lane you have a massive crush on him if you don't shut up," Harper threatened when she turned on her.

Delilah's eyes practically bugged out of her head and she shook her head fiercely. "God, no. Please don't."

"Why? Because it's true?" Delilah parted her lips, surely ready to deny it all, and Harper pointed at her. "Don't deny it. I'm serious. That whole ideal-man description you gave me last night? It's like every characteristic that makes up Lane Gallagher, I swear."

Delilah's lips clamped shut, but she lucked out at that precise moment, what with the waitress showing up with their breakfast. She dumped their plates in front of them, then buzzed off to take the next table's order. The place was starting to pick up, so Harper figured she could forgive her for the shoddy service, but whatever.

That would never happen at the BFD.

Harper grabbed the salt and sprinkled a bunch on her eggs and hash browns. After an invigorating night of awesome sex, she had quite the appetite this morning. She remembered fondly when West tried to eat *her* whole last night. Talk about awesome. She'd like a repeat performance of that particular moment sometime soon. But that was all she wanted. A fun naked romp and nothing more. That's all they could be and she was fine with it.

Really.

Her mouth watered smelling that pile of delicious-looking bacon on her plate. God, she was downright ravenous. And not really caring much about the calorie count either. "Go ahead and deny it. I dare you. At least I'm brave enough to tell you what's going on with me and West."

"Fine." Delilah dumped a bunch of syrup on her waffles and then viciously cut off a piece, popping it into her mouth. "You can't tell Wren though," she said, her mouth still full.

Great. Now they were both scared to confess to their friend that they were hot for her brothers. Worse, Harper actually had *sex* with West. Really good, amazing, mind-blowing, delicious sex that she wanted to have again. Soon.

Wren was going to kill her.

"I won't," Harper promised solemnly. "Though I guess eventually we're going to need to confess to her."

Delilah said nothing. Harper knew her friend didn't want to confess anything to Wren and guess what? Neither did she.

"So what should I do now?" Harper asked, lowering her voice. She didn't want West and Lane to overhear them. They were nearby, but not close enough to hear their murmured conversation.

"Do about what?"

Rolling her eyes, Harper tipped her head in West's direction.

"Ah." Delilah nodded, lowering her voice as well. "You act like you don't want to talk to him."

She knew she was supposed to play the nonchalant card, but he was right there. They were in the same room, he came over to talk to her, and now she was supposed to pretend he didn't exist?

"I'm not much of a game player," she admitted.

Delilah raised one dark brow. "Clearly."

"Right. And your game-playing skills have gotten you *so* far."

Delilah remained quiet for so long that Harper gave up on their conversation and started to eat her breakfast in earnest. Focusing on her food versus the man who sat nearby. She could practically feel his gaze on her.

Don't look. Don't look. Don't look!

She didn't. And she was so proud of herself it was almost ridiculous.

"He's staring at you," Delilah finally said minutes later. "Like he couldn't care less if you know he's watching you or not."

"Really?" Hope filled her but she told herself to get over it. She was being foolish.

"Oh yeah." Delilah smiled. "He's looking at you like he wants to eat you whole."

Harper gave up on her breakfast and tossed her napkin on the table beside her almost finished plate. "I'm going to the restroom," she told Delilah as she stood. "Be right back."

The restaurant was so old and out of date the restrooms were outside. Harper headed through the side door and into the chilly women's bathroom, handling her business quick before she washed her hands, scrubbing extra hard with the harsh hand soap to get the bacon stench out of her skin. She loved breakfast, but the scent always lingered on her clothes and skin long after she ate.

Pushing open the door, she stopped short when she found West standing there, waiting for her. His hands rested on his hips, the breeze ruffling his hair, making him look extra attractive, and she tried to fight the erratic beating of her heart at seeing him waiting for her. Little ol', unimportant her. But it was too late.

Her heart had taken off at an extraordinary speed, making it hard for her to speak, typical behavior for her whenever she was in West's presence.

She really needed to get over that.

Chapter Eleven

WEST COULDN'T FREAKING take it anymore. He'd sat patiently with his brother and pretended to engage in conversation, all the while keeping an eye on the beautiful woman who sat at a different table. The very woman he'd been inside of last night. The one who'd clutched him close when she came, who'd walked out on him when it was all over like she didn't give a shit about him or what they'd just done.

It had driven him crazy. He'd hardly slept last night. When Lane texted at the butt crack of dawn that he wanted to grab breakfast before he started his shift for the day, West had jumped all over it, needing the distraction.

And there she appeared, the very distraction he wanted to forget about sitting in a booth with Delilah, beautiful in her well-fucked, blissed-out state thanks to him. For the first time since he could remember, he thanked God above for living in a small town. It gave him more opportunities to see Harper.

When she got up to use the bathroom and he started to stand, Lane gave him a withering look that stopped him in his tracks. "What?"

"Are you going to chase after her?"

"Hell, yes." He'd mentioned briefly what happened between him and Harper last night to Lane.

"Do you really want to seem that eager?" Lane asked.

"I really don't care." He rose from his chair and strode across the restaurant, ignoring Delilah's watchful eyes as he passed.

She had to know. Had Harper really given her all the dirty details about what happened? Christ, he hoped not. He didn't need his old ex knowing how he performed sexually. Not that they'd ever actually had sex...

West wiped a hand across his face as he pushed open the side door that led to the outside bathrooms. He really hated the interlocking relationships that happened between his family and friends. They were like a freaking reality television show gone straight to hell.

He paced outside the two restroom doors labeled Men and Women as he waited for her, his mind racing. What if Harper had told Delilah everything? Did that mean he couldn't trust her to be discreet? He didn't want to keep what happened last night a secret, but he wanted to keep it quiet for a little while at least. Once everyone found out they were seeing each other—that sounded a lot nicer than fucking around—it would become the talk of the town.

Gossip—that was the one bad thing about living in a small town.

The women's bathroom door finally creaked open, Harper stopping short when she saw him standing there. He stopped pacing and she took a step toward him, the door slamming closed behind her. She smiled at him, the wind whipping strands of hair across her face.

Damn. He wanted to haul her in close and kiss the hell out of her. Drag her back to his place, where they could spend the rest of the day naked. In his bed. "Seeing each other."

"Hi," she said, her voice soft. "Um, are you waiting for me?"

"Did you tell Delilah what happened?" He shoved his hands in his pockets, wishing for some damn self-control for once in his life. Why'd he have to go and blurt out his question like that?

"She knows," Harper admitted, making a cute little irritated face. "I didn't give her many details, but…yeah."

He blew out a harsh breath and started pacing again. "Great. Hope she can keep her mouth shut."

"Does Lane know?" she asked.

He stopped pacing, feeling like a jackass. "Well. Yeah."

"Then we're even. Don't worry about Delilah. She won't say anything. She has her own secrets to keep."

Now his curiosity was piqued. "Oh yeah? Like what?"

"I can't tell." Harper shook her head, her pretty lips pulled tight.

"Is it that she's hot for my brother?" At the mildly horrified expression that crossed Harper's face, West snapped his fingers and pointed at her. "I freaking knew it."

"Right? It's so obvious!" She rushed toward him, her eyes dancing, like they were both in on a big secret. "Yet neither of them can see it."

"Exactly. And they won't do anything about it either." He touched her. He couldn't resist, had been dying to do it since he first saw her. Pushing a wild strand of hair away from her face, he tucked it behind her ear, his fingers lingering on her skin. "You look pretty this morning, Harper."

"I'm still wearing my makeup from last night." She pointed at her eyes, which were still rimmed with eyeliner. "I collapsed into bed once I got home and forgot to take it off."

"Slept all right?" She had the lightest smattering of freckles across the bridge of her nose. He wanted to count them. With his lips.

"Amazing." She smiled. "Crazy what a night of sex does for you."

"So it was good?" What the hell? Had he turned into an insecure kid who needed constant reassuring that what they shared had been good enough for her? That she was satisfied? Yeah, she'd come two times so she better say she was satisfied.

"You know it was good, but if you need to hear it again…" She stepped even closer to him, settling her hands on his shoulders and rising on tiptoe so she could whisper in his ear. "It was really, really good last night, West. Like, the best I've ever had."

Smiling, he slipped his arm around her waist and dipped his head, pressing his mouth to her neck. Fuck, her smell was addictive. He couldn't get enough of it. Couldn't get enough of her. "I can give you more if you'd like."

She withdrew from him, her hands dropping from his shoulders, regret etched all over her face. "Oh, I have to work today. Sorry."

Damn it, his arms felt empty without her in them. "How about later? After you're done with work?"

"I don't know." She shrugged. "I'm not sure how long it's going to take for me to clean out that office. I'm determined to get it done in two weeks. Everyone who works at the BFD laughed at me when I said that, and I'm dying to prove them wrong."

He admired her determination, but he'd much prefer if she said screw it and came home with him instead. He had nothing planned today. The weather was nice, if a little warm, and there was a breeze. The makings of fire weather, though it was still too early in the summer to do any serious damage—or so he hoped. With the drought conditions, anything could happen. "It's my last day off. I go back on shift tomorrow morning."

"Aw." She frowned. "So I won't see you for the next four days?"

"Yep." Unless she wanted to come by the station and hang out with him one evening? Maybe? Visitors were allowed though they had to understand that a call could come in at any time.

But he didn't make the offer. Bad enough what he'd said so far, looking totally desperate by trying to convince her to see him again.

"Hmm." She rested her hands on her hips, contemplating him. "Have you ever had sex in the shower, West?"

Jesus, where did she come up with this shit? More like where did his sweet little Harper get the nerve to ask such bold questions? "Um, would you like to have sex in the shower, Harper?"

She nodded, her smile blossoming, making his stomach get all jumpy. She looked at him like that and he wanted nothing more than to sling her over his shoulder and haul her off somewhere private. "I'll probably be really dirty after digging around in my grandma's office all day."

"I'm sure," he drawled, smiling.

"And I'll need someone to get all those hard-to-reach places. You know the ones I'm talking about." She went to him again, pressing a lingering kiss to his cheek. He turned his head at the last minute, their lips meeting, and he took the kiss deeper, sliding his tongue in her mouth, needing to get a taste of her. Just one. So he could have something to carry with him for the rest of the day. The memory of Harper's lips. Harper's smile. The way Harper felt in his arms.

"Whatever you need me to do, I'm here for you," he murmured against her lips after he broke the kiss. "Soap your back, wash your hair. I'm real good in a shower."

"I bet you are." She withdrew from him again, smiling as she started to back away. "I should go back inside and check on Delilah. Make sure she hasn't ditched me for Lane."

"Yeah right. Don't know if that's ever going to happen," he teased.

"Hey, you never know. I'm sure no one thought *we* could happen."

Before he could say anything in return she was gone, slipping back into the restaurant without a word. He waited a few minutes, checking his phone, studying the sky. There were big white thunderclouds forming around the nearby mountains that didn't look good. Any thunder brought with it dangerous lightning and one strike could cause a raging fire high up in the mountains. Something he definitely didn't want to deal with.

Giving up the pretense of standing around outside, he reentered the restaurant and joined Lane at their table, where his breakfast was waiting for him. Lane was already mostly finished and he glared as West dived right in.

"What did you do? Fuck her on the bathroom counter?" he asked snidely.

West glared. "Shut the hell up." A hesitation. "And for the record if I'm going to fuck a girl on a bathroom counter, I'm not choosing this place to do it. Plus, I can last longer than that."

"Right." Lane snorted. "Excuse me for insulting your sexual skills, little brother."

"We shouldn't even be having this conversation," West muttered as he munched on a piece of bacon. He watched Harper out of the corner of his eye as the two women paid their bill and rose from their table, Delilah making her way toward them and Harper falling into step behind her.

Nice. He was getting another chance to talk to Harper before she took off for the BFD. And he'd get another glimpse of Delilah flirting with the oblivious Lane. That shit was starting to become amusing.

"Just wanted to say good-bye," Delilah said, her gaze lingering on Lane in his uniform. West wouldn't be surprised if her tongue lolled out of the side of her mouth. "You going into work, Lane?"

"Yeah." He wiped his mouth with his napkin and tossed it on top of his empty plate. "What are you up to today, Dee?"

She didn't even flinch when he called her by her old and much-hated nickname. That was a sure sign she was totally hung up on his big brother. "Nothing much. It's my day off. I suppose I should go over to your sister's place and check up on her."

"What's wrong with Wren?" West asked, frowning.

"Stomach bug. Said she was barfing last night."

Ew. He was avoiding his sister at all costs.

After all, he had a shower-sex date later tonight. He didn't want anything to ruin his chances at getting Harper naked again.

HARPER TEXTED WEST right before she left the diner, going against her better judgment but deciding fairly quickly to hell with it. She may have started out playing games with West, what with the way she screwed and dashed last night, but tonight, she wasn't in the mood for games. She wanted to see him. Take him up on his self-proclaimed shower skills and see if he was as good as he said. Her muscles ached and her back was sore from working in the office today. She was seriously looking forward to having his hands on her.

Want to meet at your place around seven?

She sent the text, chewing on her lower lip as she waited for a reply. But none came. Not immediately, not after five minutes, not after fifteen.

Giving up, she hopped in her car and drove back to her grandma's place, trying her best not to get mad.

"What are you doing here?" Grandma asked the moment she walked in the house. "I thought you were going out tonight."

Frowning, Harper dumped her purse on the kitchen counter. She'd never told her grandma that. "I might go out later."

"Hmph." Her grandma shook her head. "I sort of need you out of here tonight, Harp."

Harper frowned. She couldn't remember the last time someone called her *Harp*. And she had a feeling her grandma had said it with a hint of irritation in her voice too. "Are you having company?" She braced herself for the answer.

"As a matter of fact, I am. Maybe you should go visit your parents and see what they're up to. I bet they'd love to have you over for dinner," she suggested.

Yeah right. More like they'd love to trap Harper at the dinner table and drill her about the reasons she'd broken it off with Roger. Forget that. She'd been avoiding her parents as much as possible since the relationship ended. She knew she couldn't run away from her problems forever, but for now, she liked living in her protective little bubble.

"I'll dig up plans with someone," she muttered as she went to her room, closing the door behind her.

She glanced around the tiny guest room she was temporarily calling her own, wishing she had her own place. Not that she could afford anything by herself. She'd definitely need a roommate to survive on the money she was currently making. Delilah had offered her couch in her tiny one-bedroom apartment on the second floor of her dance studio, but Harper had declined. And Wren lived in a small, one-room cottage on the far edge of her parents' property, close to the lake. She hadn't even bothered offering Harper a place to crash because she knew Harper would say no.

Considering how isolated Wren's place was, it actually gave Harper the creeps anyway so…no thanks.

She had her phone clutched in her hand, her gaze stuck on the screen as she silently demanded West to text her back.

As if by magic, her phone lit up with a text message from him. But when she read it, the disappointment made her shoulders deflate.

Sorry. Got called back to the station to cover. Can I get a rain check on that shower?

Wow, there went her evening plans for real.

Everything okay? Is there a big fire or something?

Her phone buzzed in her hand.

Yeah. Tate's engine got called out on a strike team. Big fire near Sacramento. I'm stuck here covering. No days off in the foreseeable future.

She pressed her lips together, staring at West's text. Firefighters worked lots of overtime and during the summer months, the Cal Fire guys worked constantly.

But West said he was at the station. He hadn't been called out on a fire. So maybe...

Want some company? Or are you not allowed visitors?

Hitting Send before she chickened out was the only way to go. She sat on the edge of the bed and chewed on a fingernail while she waited for his reply. Where had her it's-just-sex attitude gone?

Right out the freaking window.

Yeah you should stop by and see me. If you want. No shower time though.

Harper smiled, liking how he added the *if you want.* Please. She so wanted. But she needed to play it cool. Not behave like an overeager slobbery dog.

I could stop by for a little while I suppose.

There. That was perfect. Making the offer but not saying *please let me move in with you!* That would just reek of desperation. And she didn't want to move in with him. Despite the fact that he was living in her former home and she'd give anything to crash the spare bedroom there so she wouldn't have to deal with her grandma kicking her out on a Saturday night so she could entertain her gentleman friend.

Otherwise known as her grandma's hookup. Yikes.

Her phone dinged.

You suppose? Sure it wouldn't put you out to come all the way out here?

The station was on the opposite end of town, but she was willing to drive all that way to spend a little quality time with West, even if it wasn't private.

I'm sure.

She hesitated, then decided to go for it.

Plus I'd like to see where you work.

Meaning she'd like to see him, if only for an hour. Sitting around in his uniform. Looking sexy. Offering up one of those secret smiles that drove her a little crazy with wanting him.

He didn't hesitate answering her at all.

Then come by around eight.

Smiling, she tapped out her two-letter response:

Ok. ☺

Chapter Twelve

HARPER TOOK A shower. She washed her hair, spent almost thirty minutes blowing it dry, and even curled the ends with her two-hundred-dollar curling iron. Yeah, that silly curling iron had been a huge expense but well worth the purchase. Her twice-a-year excursions to Sephora were some of her favorite shopping experiences.

Taking into consideration the weather, her outfit was chosen with care—white denim shorts and a red tank top that clung to her boobs nicely, if she did say so herself. Subtle makeup and a slick of that same red lipstick she'd worn last night to seduce him completed the look.

And her efforts proved worth the time. The moment she exited her car and West first saw her, his appreciative gaze started a warm, downright manic flutter in her stomach.

"Aren't you a sight for sore eyes?" That slow, syrupy drawl of a voice washed over her as he swept her into his arms. That she was plastered up against her car made her want to laugh. He hadn't let her get two steps before he had her pinned.

She rested her hands on his chest, momentarily preventing his lips from settling on hers. "What if someone sees us?"

He frowned, a little crease appearing between his eyebrows. That was so cute. Pretty much everything he did was cute, even when he looked put out. "Who cares? They're all inside anyway."

His casual *who cares* remark threw her, allowing him the kissing advantage. He settled his mouth on hers, slow and easy, her eyes sliding shut as he proceeded to kiss every rational thought out of her brain.

Oh, boy. This could become a real addiction, real quick.

Admiring his uniform shirt, she ran her hands down the front of his chest when he broke away from her lips. There was a shiny gold name badge pinned on the right side of his chest, right above the pocket. She slowly traced the letters, could feel him watching her, and it made her feel shy.

So incredibly silly.

"Weston Gallagher." Harper glanced up at him, saw the way his gaze dropped to her mouth. Looked like he had a one-track mind tonight. "Did you ever think you'd be back here in Wildwood, Weston Gallagher?"

He shook his head, leaning in to kiss her again, but she dodged him. Once they started that she wouldn't want to stop and nothing was happening tonight at the station.

She could guarantee that. His magic lips may cause her to lose all rational thought, but they were at his workplace. No way would she ever do something scandalous with him while he was on duty.

Well. She didn't think she would…

"This was the last place I expected to find myself," he admitted, rerouting his intent and burying his face against her neck. She closed her eyes and wrapped her arms around him, pulling him in as close as she could get him. Just for a few seconds. Just so she could savor being in his arms.

"Are you glad you're back?" She held her breath, not only because he was nibbling her earlobe, but also because she waited for his answer.

"Yeah. There are a lot of benefits to being back in Wildwood." He lifted his head, smiling at her before he went in for another quick kiss.

She let him have it this time. She never claimed she was any good at using restraint. "Such as?" she asked, blinking up at him. Would he say her? No, he couldn't say her. That was expecting too much. Way, way too much.

And she needed to remember that she expected nothing but a good time from West.

He skimmed calloused fingers across her cheek, tucked a few strands of hair behind her ear, his gentle touch making her shiver. His hands were rough, a real man's hands. A workingman's hands, not a soft accountant-type hand in sight. Oh, she really, really liked those hands of his, especially when they were on her. "You're pretty high up on that benefits list, Harper."

Her heart did a dramatic tumble in her chest, landing somewhere in the vicinity of her stomach. "So no regrets, Mr. Gallagher?" Why was she pretending to be some sort of demented reporter? And why was she asking him questions with answers that scared her?

"None whatsoever so far." He kissed her again, taking this one deeper. Longer. Helping her get lost in the sensual sweeps of his tongue, the way his fingers tangled up in her hair, his other hand sliding over her butt, back and forth, nudging her closer and closer.

"West," she whispered against his lips, trying to get him to stop. "We need to slow down." Not just the kissing, but…everything. He knew just how to sweep her off her feet, but she couldn't get too caught up. This was just sex with West. That was it.

Just. Sex.

"The hell we do." He tilted his head, changing the angle of their kiss, and she tried to shove him away. She needed a clear head.

"I'm serious." She curled her hand into a fist and rapped it against the center of his chest, trying to fend him off. But he wasn't budging. Of course he wasn't budging. He was built like one of those towering pines that circled Wildwood. Tall and imposing and freaking impossible to move. "There will be no freaky business happening at this station."

He started to laugh. It was such a nice sound, rich and inviting. She remembered back in high school when he would laugh often, the sound so infectious that people would swarm around him, desperate to get near him, be his friend, his girlfriend, whatever. She'd never been lucky enough to be one of the coveted few who'd moved through life in West Gallagher's social circle. Oh, she'd been closer to him than most, but being the best friend of his sister hadn't really counted back then.

She definitely remembered wishing for something more, for something like what they were sharing at this very exact moment. Firmly believing back then that what she yearned for was nothing but a fairy tale, a pipe dream, pie in the freaking sky.

Whatever that saying meant. She should probably do a Google search on that later…

Taking a deep breath, she tried to keep it together.

Okay. Focusing.

"Next you'll tell me there will be no hanky-panky." When she didn't say anything he continued, looking perplexed. "My parents always used that saying. I thought it was dumb."

She could beat him. "My parents called it *getting frisky*. After a while, that just got embarrassing." So incredibly embarrassing. But her parents had insisted that was their purpose in life—giving their kids as much grief as possible and making their life a living hell of constant embarrassment.

"I think we should bring it back." There went his mouth again, brushing against hers with infinite, excruciatingly slow care. "Getting frisky. I love it."

"You do not," she mumbled against his mouth, a gasp escaping her when he licked—*licked*—her lips. Right there in the parking lot of the Wildwood fire station. He'd lost his mind.

Well, so had she so at least they were equal.

"Your tank top is ruining me for life," he said as he rested both of his hands on her waist and slowly brought them up. Up. Until they rested just beneath her breasts, touching them but not really. More like a ghost of a touch, eliciting a phantom of a feeling.

All the breath caught in her throat, but somehow she managed to talk. "What do you mean?"

"Red and sexy, revealing just the slightest hint of cleavage without being blatant. The fabric clinging to your curves so I can see exactly how hard your nipples are." He was leaning in. Yet again, the persistent man, but she dipped her head down to check out said nipples only to find them announcing to anyone who was looking that they were very, extremely hard. Damn her too-thin bra.

"A gentleman wouldn't look," she chastised primly, hoping he could possibly stay a gentleman for a few more minutes so God and anybody else on shift at the station wouldn't see her getting felt up by their man in charge.

"I never said I was a gentleman, Harper. You of all people should know that." His amused tone was undeniable. As in, she couldn't deny that she found every word that fell from his lips charming. Each way that he touched her, she wanted to find another way, and yet another way, again and again, in order to keep him keep on touching her.

"Why did you kiss me that night?" she asked just as he started running his lips along the side of her neck.

West lifted his head to look at her, his gaze full of confusion. "What night are you talking about?" His tone was casual. Too casual. He knew exactly what night she was referring to.

"The night before you packed your bags and escaped Wildwood supposedly for good," she reminded him, poking his chest with her index finger.

His expression went from neutral to miserable in a split second. "I was a jackass that night."

"Totally." Well. She'd had the time of her life that night. It was the next morning when she'd gotten so angry, when she discovered that he'd left without a good-bye. Kiss and run, that was West's specialty.

"You were just so pretty and sweet and looking at me with those big eyes of yours and…" His voice drifted.

"And?" she asked when he remained silent for too long.

"And I couldn't resist you. I wanted just one taste." He tried to kiss her again, but she dodged him. "Once I had a taste, I wanted another. And another. You never protested."

She couldn't protest, not when it came to West.

"I've always felt like shit for ditching you like that," he admitted.

Dropping her gaze from his, she traced her index finger over his badge, trying her best to keep her composure. "It hurt, how you left. You never tried to contact me. Ever."

"I was an asshole." He blew out a ragged breath. "I'm sorry."

"You're still an asshole." A sexy asshole. She curled her hand into a fist and lightly pounded the center of his chest. "But I forgive you."

He slipped his fingers beneath her chin, tilting her face up so her gaze met his. "Really?"

Harper nodded but remained silent. Her throat was suddenly clogged with all the words she couldn't say.

"Thank Christ," he muttered just before he kissed her. Soft and slow and deliberate. He used his lips like weapons to obliterate all of her thoughts, her every possible protest.

Whatever they were experiencing, this particular encounter—all of their encounters, really—couldn't go any further. Nothing beyond the casual, oh let's screw around and get it out of our system type of thing.

And she definitely wasn't going to let anything happen between them tonight. There were people who worked for him inside the barracks and he could get a call at any minute. She refused to let him feel her up or try to take her clothes off while they were outside pressed up against her car like two horny teenagers ready to go at it whatever chance they got.

They were older now and more mature. They had homes. Careers. Lives.

Well, not really, at least not in your case. You're crashing at your grandma's and West is paying rent on your old condo.

Huh.

And your so-called career is in the toilet. What do you plan on doing once you're done cleaning out the office at the BFD? Do you even know?

Harper frowned. Maybe she didn't know. And who cared? She certainly didn't. Not that she wanted to become dependent on a man and sweep his floors barefoot while a baby rested on her hip. No freaking way was she looking for something like that.

She needed a man who believed in modern things, who used his brain for good and not for evil, who wanted nothing more but to take care of her, all the while believing in her to go out into the world and kick its ass.

Could West be that man?

Nah. Probably not. He said so himself that he wasn't relationship material. But did he still think that way though? Besides, didn't it sort of hurt, that she couldn't have something...real with him?

No. She wanted easy and casual, and that's what she was getting. There was no need to raise her expectations. Lowering them was smarter. For once, she needed to guard her heart.

Not lay it all out only for it to get smashed to bits.

WHILE WEST HAD no problem appreciating a beautiful woman, he could usually keep his hands to himself, especially at work.

He'd seen a few of his fellow employees lose their shit over women over the years. One captain he worked for had had a sweet, unsuspecting wife at home and a trashy girlfriend who'd visit him while he was on shift. They'd disappear nightly—rumor had it she'd given him blowjobs out back behind the garage.

Yeah. That entire scenario had disgusted him. Rumor also had it that his own father had had a few illicit affairs himself back in the day. His parents' marriage had been on shaky ground at one point. But somehow, his mother had forgiven his dad and taken him back. Their relationship was stronger than ever.

But based on that tumultuous moment in his parents' marriage, West's view on relationships had been forever skewed. His feelings about his father were forever altered too, not that the old man cared too much. They still hadn't spent any time together since West returned to Wildwood. Claimed he was too busy fishing out in his boat.

Figured his father would rather fish alone out on the lake than see his son. Not that West really wanted to see him either.

He'd never had a woman visit him while he was at the station. He'd never *wanted* a woman to visit him. Seemed best to keep his work and personal relationships separate, thank you very much. Yet seeing Harper when she emerged from her car wearing those tiny shorts and that clingy tank top had turned him into a slobbering fool. His hands had literally itched to get on her. And once they had, he still wasn't satisfied. He wanted more.

He wanted naked.

Breathing deep, he tucked her close to him and glanced around, thankful no one was outside. They were all in the barracks, hanging out in the commons area and watching a movie. Ice-cream sundaes were being prepared when he'd gone outside to meet Harper and, while he could appreciate hot fudge sauce as much as the next guy, for once in his life he wasn't thinking with his stomach.

Instead, he was thinking with his unusually needy dick. Not the smartest move on his part. But one look at Harper smiling shyly at him, hot as hell with all that exposed skin, and he'd been a goner.

A goner with a slight boner—that was a reckless combo. And there was the root of his problem. Harper made him feel reckless. Careless. A few days ago he had firmly told himself he couldn't touch her. A few weeks ago he'd been pissed that he was in Wildwood in the first place.

Now he was thankful to be back in his hometown because it meant that Harper was there too. And he'd not only touched her, he'd had his hands all over her, his fingers inside her, and oh yeah, his cock too. He wanted that again. Soon.

If he hadn't been called into work, he'd be doing it— *her*—right now. Talk about feeling resentful. And when she brought up their first kiss from so long ago? The night he both idealized and regretted, all at once? He'd broken out in a nervous sweat, too damn afraid she'd tell him to go to hell and run out on him once and for all.

He deserved her resentment. Why she'd given him another chance, he wasn't sure. But he wasn't about to question it either.

"What's going on with that fire?" Harper asked.

West blinked, trying to recall exactly which fire she could be referring to. Oh yeah…

"Ten thousand acres and only eight percent contained." At the shocked look on Harper's face he continued. "It's in El Dorado County, lots of rolling hills and forest up there. It's all so dry it's igniting with a snap of a finger."

"That's awful," she murmured against his chest.

"Most of the land is unpopulated. No structures have been threatened beyond a couple of old barns," he reassured her, giving her a squeeze. He liked the way she felt in his arms. Probably liked it too much, but he couldn't analyze that right now.

He didn't want to freak himself out.

"So Tate's out on the fire?"

"Yeah. We sent a strike team up there and Tate's engine was included."

West usually loved being called out on a strike team. Providing coverage for a complex fire meant he'd be gone for days, sometimes weeks at a time. And that meant the dollars just kept rolling in. All that overtime money he made over the years had gone straight into his savings account.

But that had been when he was a firefighter. Now that he was a limited-term engineer, he was on a different pay structure. He'd received a decent promotion and pay raise, but it was calculated in another way now. Something he was still adjusting to.

But now he was relieved that he didn't have to go out on that call. Not like he could go home either what with the station being short on coverage, but at least he wasn't gone.

At least he had Harper snug in his arms.

"Hey, how are you adjusting to your new position?" Harper asked, pushing him out of his thoughts.

Ah, and she was a mind reader.

"I like it here. It's familiar. And I like everyone I work with. Tate's a good guy. I could see us becoming friends." He was surprised he'd admit that much to her, but it was true. And he'd never had a problem opening up to Harper. He just wasn't good opening up with regards to the feelings he *had* for Harper.

And didn't thinking that just make him stand a little straighter?

"He's an awesome guy. Everyone likes him a lot around here. He's a good fit," she agreed.

Jealousy reared its ugly head and he tamped it down. He was being ridiculous, though really, Tate was an all-around perfect motherfucker. Good-looking, strong, smart, fast; he had all the guys laughing and all the girls swooning. West should sort of hate him. But the dude was so damn nice, he couldn't help but like him.

"You like him that much, huh?" He heard the surliness in his tone. He sounded like a jealous asshole. Like he had any right to be jealous. Harper wasn't his. Not really.

"He's very nice," she said diplomatically, her fingers sliding along his shoulder, down the length of his right arm. "You should tell me about your tattoos."

"What about them?" The first one had been a moment of rebellion. The rush of pain he got when the needle was on his skin soon became an addiction. Plus, a few of his previous supervisors hadn't approved of them, which had only spurred him on to get more. When he first visited his parents upon returning to Wildwood, his dad nearly had a shit fit when he saw them.

Made West want to go out and get more, which was ridiculous. Something about his father's constant nagging and disapproval made him want to rebel. He'd always wanted to rebel. Causing trouble was the name of the game for so damn long, he'd had a hard time pushing himself out of the role.

"Some of them are unusual. Like, I understand why you got this one." Her fingers skimmed the flames on his bicep. "But why the others? Like this one?" She touched the center of a rose, tracing the delicate flowers.

He shrugged, suddenly uncomfortable. Maybe it wasn't easier with Harper after all? Old habits were hard to break. He wasn't one to explain his actions or choices. "I thought it looked cool." She smiled but said nothing, making him curious. "What?"

"I thought there would be some epic reason for your ink." She lifted her head so their gazes met. "Maybe some girl broke your heart."

He chuckled. "Hell no."

She nudged his chest with two fingers. "No girl has ever broken your heart?"

"You looking for information, Harper?" he teased. At her solemn expression he turned serious too. "No. I've never put my heart on the line so it's never had a chance to be broken."

"Oh."

West slipped his fingers beneath her chin and tilted her face up. He didn't like that sad little "oh." Why, he wasn't sure. What did it matter?

Harper actually matters to you, that's why. You like her. You've known her a long time. She deserves respect, not just a quick fuck.

"Putting myself out there isn't always easy for me," he said. "I'm not a fan of rejection. I've also had too much happening in my life, mostly with work. I wasn't ready for a relationship." *Yet.*

West frowned.

Harper actually snorted. "Okay. Whatever."

He tried his best not to get irritated, but…shit. It was the truth. "Hey. It's a valid reason."

"I guess." She sent him a skeptical look. "I think sometimes people are just scared."

"Scared of what?" He frowned down at her.

"Commitment. Love." Her smile went a little dreamy, making her extremely dangerous.

That was the look of a woman who had no fear whatsoever of either. Usually those types of women were his darkest nightmare.

But when it came to Harper, he might be willing to change his mind.

Chapter Thirteen

HARPER WAS AT the Bigfoot Diner, cleaning out yet another filing cabinet drawer and wondering what sort of excuse she could come up with to bail out of this place early when she heard a familiar voice.

"Girls only tonight."

Harper opened her mouth, fully prepared to protest, but Delilah cut her off.

"No arguing, it's happening. Wren and I will come pick you up tonight at your grandma's. Wear your sparkliest top and your tightest jeans."

Harper frowned, leaning back in her grandma's old office chair and making it squeak. "But I don't have any sparkly tops."

Delilah waved her hand, an irritated scowl on her face. She stood in the open doorway of the BFD office, wearing a tiny pair of black booty shorts and a hot pink bra top, her long hair pulled up into a perfect bun. In other words,

Delilah looked pretty amazing. She must've just finished with a dance class. "Whatever. Wear something cute. No, make that something *sexy*. We're going to that new bar-restaurant place out by the lake."

"What new restaurant?" Oh, wait. Delilah was talking about that one place, the two-story building with the bar on the top floor and the restaurant on the bottom. It had recently come under new ownership and they'd spent the entire winter remodeling it. They'd had their grand reopening just last week. "I shouldn't go there," Harper said before Delilah could say anything else. "They're the enemy."

"Please. They're trying to pull in a totally different crowd and you know it." Delilah rested her hands on her hips, emphasizing just how slender she was, making Harper more than a little bit jealous. "Think of it this way—you could totally spy on them and report back to your grandma. All while picking up hot single men."

Harper made a face. Picking up supposedly hot single men was the last thing she wanted to do. She already had one. Sort of. It had been days since she'd seen West. Tate's engine was still on that fire up near Sacramento and they'd left almost a week ago, which meant that West still hadn't gotten a day off. And he went out on every single call that the Wildwood station received. The other station on the outskirts of town where Holden worked was down an engine too. In other words, West was really busy.

She missed him. A lot. And now here was Delilah, who knew full well she had a thing—what else could she call it?—with West, trying to get her to go out on a manhunt?

It made no sense.

"I don't want to pick up hot single men," Harper said, watching as Delilah stepped into the office and shut the door behind her. Good, privacy so she could say what was really holding her up. "I'm sort of seeing West, remember?"

"It's that *sort of seeing him* line that makes me question it." Delilah flopped down in the chair on the other side of the desk. "We should just forget those Gallagher men ever existed, I swear. They're so stupid they couldn't see the truth if it came up and smacked them in the face."

Uh-oh. "What's going on?" Harper asked gently. Yeah, she hadn't seen West in a few days and that was frustrating, but at least she knew they were on the same page.

Well. She was fairly certain they were on the same page.

Were they?

God, she hated feeling so doubtful. She didn't want anything serious and she believed West felt the same way. But then she'd catch herself thinking…commitment-type thoughts. And those were pointless so she'd banish them.

Only to have them come back full force when West texted her something sweet or when he sent her a photo of the cat he rescued from a tree. That had happened earlier today, the pretty tabby cat looking ready to leap out of his arms as West grinned for the camera.

Yeah. He didn't make things easy, not that she was surprised. She always knew West was the best kind of complicated.

"Lane." Delilah blew out a harsh breath and rolled her eyes. She said his name like it was a bad word. "He came by the studio earlier."

"Okay. And?" Harper prodded.

"And I was all alone. I had a half-hour lunch break before the next class came and for some weird reason, no one else was in the studio. Trust me, that *never* happens. There are always girls hanging around." Delilah slowly shook her head. "So we started flirting. I told him he should bring me lunch next time he stopped by and he said he didn't know what I liked."

Well, that didn't sound so awful to Harper.

"And then I told him he knew *exactly* what I liked." Delilah sent her a pointed look. "He played dumb and told me he had no idea what I was talking about."

"Maybe he didn't?" Harper suggested. "Sometimes men are completely clueless." And that was the God's honest truth.

"Trust me, he knew. He had to know I was referring to *him*! If not, he's an idiot. I swear to God, he acts like I terrify him most of the time." The disgust in Delilah's voice was clear.

"I think you might," Harper said, making Delilah laugh. "I'm serious. Poor guy probably didn't know what hit him, what with you coming at him strong."

"I don't know why he has to act like we can't even flirt with each other. He's always hands-off, all the time," Delilah said irritably. "I'm giving up on him, I swear. Tonight, we're going out and having fun and meeting new guys. Wren is in. I talked to her on the way here."

"But what about—"

"No *buts*. No protests. I don't care if you're banging West, you're coming out with us tonight." Delilah stood.

"Besides, who knows how long this thing will last. They don't know the meaning of the word *commitment*."

Harper couldn't get over how casually Delilah had said she was banging West, like it was no big deal. It was a *huge* deal to her. She didn't *just bang* guys. She'd had a thing for West for years.

But if she was being truthful, that's exactly what she was doing. Banging West. Not that they'd done much banging, what with him being stuck at the station working overtime.

"Hey, don't project your issues with Lane onto my relationship with West," Harper said, tempted to wag her finger at her friend. Seriously, the last thing she needed was Delilah putting doubts in her head. She was pretty good at that on her own.

"You're right; I'm sorry." Delilah shrugged, not looking very sorry at all. "I'm sexually frustrated. It tends to make me snippy. And overdramatic."

"No kidding," Harper muttered. "When did you want to meet tonight?"

"I'll swing by and pick you up around seven? Is that good?"

"Perfect."

The moment Delilah walked out, Harper's phone started to ring, which was unusual. Pretty much everyone who needed to talk to her texted first, including her mom. It was so much easier that way.

But when she saw who was calling her, she answered immediately. "Hey, you."

"Hi. I wanted to hear your voice." West's deep, sexy voice made her smile. And shiver. "How are you?"

"I'm good. Where are you?" *Don't get your hopes up. Don't get your hopes up.*

"Still at the station. About ready to tear my hair out. I'm so anxious to get out of here."

Her hopes crashed to the ground in a tangled heap of disappointment. "That sucks."

"Yeah, but I have good news. Maybe." He paused. "Rumor has it that Tate and his crew might be on their way back to the station today. They'll need a few days off, but another engine from a nearby station is coming over to give all of us some reprieve."

"No way," Harper breathed, excitement building inside her. She wanted to see him so bad she could hardly stand it. "That's great news."

"I know. I can't wait to sleep in my own bed. Even if it really isn't my own bed." He took a deep breath. "Used to be yours, right?"

"Right," she admitted softly, glancing up at the open doorway to double-check that no one was around. She turned the chair around so her back faced the open door. "You like sleeping in my old bed?"

"Definitely. But I'd prefer it if you were sleeping with me," he admitted in a growly whisper that filled her brain with all sorts of interesting images. "Not that we'd get much sleep."

Her heart fluttered. "Are you off tonight?" Delilah would kill her if she canceled on them, but she'd eventually understand. After all, Harper was sexually frustrated too.

One taste of West wasn't nearly enough. He made her greedy. She wanted more.

More sex. With West. That was it. Not a relationship, nothing serious. Just free and easy. That was all she
wanted.

Right?

Harper frowned. Why did she feel like she was constantly arguing with herself?

"That's the problem. I have no idea when I'm off, or
if this is really going to happen tonight. I just wanted
to keep you posted, let you know what's going on," he
explained.

She clutched the phone closer to her ear. "I'm glad you
did. Thank you for calling."

They chatted for the next few minutes, mostly about
stuff that had been happening since they saw each other
last. Harper didn't have much—cleaning out a messy
office wasn't that exciting. So she let West talk, absorbing
all of his stories, her frown deepening the more he said.

He'd gone on some dangerous calls, something she'd
never really thought about before. But he put his life at risk
to help others and that gave her a warm, fuzzy feeling inside.

"I've missed you," he finally admitted, his voice gruff.
Like he didn't want to say it but had to anyway.

"I've missed you too." She smiled and her heart
squeezed. She told herself to settle down. Feeling all
swoony over West wasn't smart. Delilah was right. How
serious could those Gallagher brothers ever really be?
They didn't do relationships. "Call or text me when you
know what's going on, okay?"

"I will."

"Be safe." She swallowed past the sudden lump in her throat, thinking again of all the dangerous things West faced on a daily basis. If they ever were to become serious, would she be able to handle it? Knowing that he put himself on the line every single day? That maybe…*oh, God*…he wouldn't come home one day?

A shudder moved through her at the horrible thought.

"You too, baby," he murmured.

Her belly was warm long after she ended the call with West. He'd called her *baby*. Like maybe she *did* mean something to him, which was probably ridiculous on her part yet…She couldn't help but think that way. They'd always had a connection. Now that they'd finally acted on that connection, maybe they really could make it work.

Or maybe they couldn't.

Frowning, she tossed her phone in her purse and tried her best to focus on anything but West while she dug back into a file folder of receipts from 2009.

But there she was. Still feeling all swoony over West Gallagher. Probably going to end up being the biggest regret of her life. But she was going to try her best to enjoy every single minute of it.

"OH MY GOD, how many people are in this place?" Harper glanced around as they stood at the top of the stairs, surprised to see how crowded the small bar area was. She spotted a few familiar faces, but mostly it was filled with tourists, beer bottles in hands and giant smiles stretching their mouths wide. They were all dressed casually, many of them looking as if they had just come off the lake, their faces shiny with sunburns, their hair windblown.

Harper felt distinctly overdressed in her floaty white top, cropped jeans, and sandals, and she'd worried she was dressed too casually. Ha. Better that she was out and not sitting at home moping after West confirmed he wasn't able to get off work tonight. Thank goodness she had alternate plans. A night alone with ice cream and her laptop didn't sound like much fun.

Loud music played, the bass throbbing, making it hard to hear. Delilah leaned in close, yelling in Harper's ear, "Look at all the good-looking guys in here!"

Wren somehow heard her over the music. "Yeah there are," she agreed with a smile. "This place is crawling with them!"

Harper nodded, hoping she looked enthusiastic, though all she saw were average-looking guys, more than a few of them studying the three women with interest.

The reality? She so didn't want to be here. But what was the option? Sitting at home alone waiting for West to call or going out with her friends, nursing the same drink all night and watching while they got their flirt on with tourists they'd never see again?

Plus, she needed to fake it for Wren's benefit. She still hadn't told her best friend in the entire world that she was, as Delilah had so thoughtfully put it earlier, *banging* her brother. She didn't know how to tell her without making what she and West were doing sound sordid and sneaky.

"Let's dance!" Delilah yelled as she dragged them onto the dance floor. Delilah started to move to the music, her movements fluid and natural, immediately making Harper feel inadequate. She knew she wasn't a crap dancer, but compared with Delilah? Forget it.

Wren kept up with Delilah, earning them more appreciative glances from the few men on the tiny dance floor near the bar. They danced one song, then two, onto three when Harper finally had to grab Delilah and tell her she was thirsty and needed a drink.

They talked about nothing in particular as they waited for the bartender to come over and take their drink order, screaming at each other over the loud music. Wren kept asking Harper what she'd been up to and she deflected, feeling like a jerk. But how could she tell her the truth?

"Oh, I've been working and pining over your brother who's stuck at work. You didn't know we've been seeing each other? Well, that's the polite way to put it. Really we've been screwing around and let me tell you, Wren, West knows how to rock my world. I think I could seriously fall for him. Like…"

Seriously.

Harper frowned. Um, she so couldn't say that.

And she hated herself for it. Not being able to dig up the guts to tell Wren, afraid that she'd be mad at her, was ridiculous. But the longer Harper kept quiet the angrier Wren would most likely be. Harper was caught in a vicious cycle that was going nowhere. And she hated it.

"Hey! We need drinks!" Wren leaned over the counter, her hand in the air as she tried to get the bartender's attention. He was too busy flirting with another group of women standing on the opposite end of the bar. All three of them wore teeny bikini tops barely covering their goods so they definitely had the advantage.

Already bored, Harper pulled her phone out of the back pocket of her jeans to check if she had a message. Maybe West had texted her to let her know he was coming home? But there was nothing. Of course.

Sighing, she slipped her phone back into her pocket, just as Delilah slid in between her and Wren, a stern look on her face.

"Listen, don't look so down in the dumps, wishing you were with your man," Delilah said, glancing over her shoulder at Wren to make sure she wasn't paying attention. But she was too busy trying to get the attention of the bartender. "She's going to ask what's up if you keep acting all sad and shit."

"I need to just tell her. She's going to find out eventually. I feel terrible that I'm keeping this from her," Harper said. "I don't like feeling like I'm lying to her." Feeling like she was lying, that was a good one. There was no *feeling* about it.

She was totally lying.

"Whatever you do, don't confess your sins with her brother tonight. The last thing I want is for you two to get into a fight. We're supposed to be having fun." Delilah grabbed Harper's shoulders and gave her a little shake. "Come on, live a little. At least your man is giving it to you."

"Your man? You have a man, Harper?"

Harper went still when she heard Wren's voice. Delilah sent her a look, then turned, the both of them facing

Wren like a united front. People crowded the bar, pushing into them, and the song blasting over the speakers switched to an upbeat country song, making everyone around them cheer in approval.

"Who's your secret lover?" Wren asked, one delicate brow arched as she stared at Harper.

Nerves ate at Harper's insides and she looked for guidance to Delilah, who was clearly sending her the *keep your mouth shut* message with her eyes.

But Harper…she couldn't do it. She had to confess. Get it off her chest.

"I'm seeing West," she said quietly, her voice so low she almost hoped Wren wouldn't hear her. Though of course, she did, even with the loud music playing.

"Wait a minute. You're seeing my *brother* West?" Wren looked from Harper to Delilah, her expression downright horrified as she pointed at Delilah. "And *you* knew before *I* did?"

"That's because she's crushing on Lane, but he won't do anything about it," Harper blurted, like she couldn't control herself. She slapped her hand over her mouth the moment she said it just as Delilah sent her a glare that could've silenced ten squirmy little ballet students on a Tuesday afternoon.

Clearly, that glare couldn't silence Harper though.

"Lane? Are you serious, Delilah?" Wren's eyes looked like they were going to bug out of her head.

"Nothing's happening between Lane and me," Delilah said in a rush, stepping toward Wren. But Wren dodged her when Delilah tried to touch her arm. "I'm serious. I had a crush on him, but it's pointless. He'll never see me as anything but a friend."

"But you want more?" Wren turned on Harper. "And you do too? With West? How could you not tell me?" Her eyes blazed with anger.

And hurt. So much hurt. Harper's heart cracked, knowing she was the one who'd done that to Wren. Her best friend since they were little kids. They never kept secrets from each other. Ever.

"We didn't know how, Wren," Harper said. Delilah snorted, but Harper ignored her. "I'm not even sure if this is going to last, you know? West isn't, um, big on commitment."

"That's a total understatement," Wren said bitterly, shaking her head. "Did you leave Roger for my flaky brother? Because if that's the case, you're an idiot. You had a nice, stable relationship with a good guy, and you break it off for a chance with West. Unbelievable. Not that I should be too surprised. You've had a thing for him since we were kids."

"I didn't break up with Roger for West. That happened on its own."

"So, what? You and West are *dating* now?" Wren actually laughed. "Let's see how long that lasts. He doesn't do long term. Delilah knows this firsthand."

That last remark stung. Harper knew Wren was mad and was just trying to make her feel bad, but still.

"And if you really think you have a chance with Lane, Dee, then you can forget it. That guy is cold. He doesn't care about anything but work," Wren practically spit out, scowling. "The only one with any heart is Holden, and he's already taken. Or are you going to chase after him too? Try your chance at all the Gallagher brothers, Dee?"

"Come on, Wren. That was a low blow," Harper started, shocked her friend would say such a thing.

Delilah stepped close to Wren, poking her in the chest with her index finger. "This is exactly why we didn't tell you. We knew you would be a total jerk about it. You've always been jealous of the attention your brothers get. You couldn't stand the thought of your friends wanting to be with them."

"That's not true," Wren said, but Delilah wasn't listening.

"I'm leaving. You coming with me, Harper?" They'd ridden together in Delilah's car and met Wren at the restaurant.

Harper met Wren's gaze. "I wish you'd understand. I really…care for your brother," she said.

"If you cared about me, you would've told me you liked him in the first place." Wren folded her arms in front of her.

"Right. And you would've told me not to waste my time." Harper had heard it all before. Wren had never encouraged her interest in West. Back in the day she'd hated that Delilah and West went out, even for a short time. She hadn't wanted her brother to sabotage her friendships all for a fleeting romantic entanglement.

"That's because it is a waste of time when it comes to West," Wren argued. "Lane too. But who am I to stand in the path of true love? Oh, I know, I'm your *best friend*."

"What is this? High school? Enough with the guilt trips. Come on, Harper." Delilah grabbed hold of her arm and practically dragged her out of the bar area, stopping when they got to the top of the stairs. "Why did you tell her when I asked you not to? I knew she'd freak out and act like a total bitch."

"Delilah, don't call her that. She's just upset," Harper chastised.

"She's upset because you opened your big mouth," Delilah muttered, her gaze going back to Wren. "She should just come home with us."

"She's too mad."

"I'm sort of mad at her, too, and I'm mad at you. Way to ruin our night out." Delilah shook her head.

Harper refused to feel bad. The guilt had been tearing her up inside. At least it was all out in the open. The worst part was over.

"Let's go," Delilah said.

Harper frowned, sniffing the air. "Is that smoke? Do you smell it?"

Delilah waved a hand, her expression irritated. "Probably someone smoking out on the deck."

Harper wrinkled her nose as she looked around the crowded room, but everyone seemed to be carrying on like no big deal. She knew she smelled smoke. Or was she imagining it? "It doesn't smell like cigarettes to me."

"Then it's probably something else. Don't worry about it, let's get out of here," Delilah grumbled as she started to go down the stairs. Harper glanced over her shoulder toward the bar area and found Wren watching her, her expression somber. She wanted to go back to her. Wanted to ask her to forgive, to understand, to say she was sorry, but she couldn't do it. Not now. Not yet.

Harper knew Wren wasn't ready to listen.

A continuous beeping sound started, sharp and piercing, making Harper immediately cover her ears. The music abruptly shut off and everyone seemed to stop talking all at once, looking at each other in confusion. That's when Harper saw it. A cloud of smoke filling the room, dark gray and thick. Someone began yelling at the top of the person's lungs.

"Fire! Run!"

"Wren!" Harper yelled, squealing when she felt someone grab hold of her arm and start to pull her down the stairs. "No, Delilah, we can't leave her!"

"We have to go!" Delilah screamed.

It was a crush of people, everyone rushing for the stairs all at once as the smoke grew thicker, making Harper cough. She took a deep breath, gasping when she felt the sharp burn fill her lungs. Someone stepped on her toes and she yelped, her left sandal slipping off her foot as she tripped down the stairs.

Delilah let go of her hand amid the people shoving and pushing around them in their haste to get down the stairs and out of the building. Harper looked behind her, hoping to spot Wren, but she couldn't find her in the crowd. And she couldn't see Delilah anymore either.

Surrounded by so many strangers as she stumbled down the stairs, her friends nowhere in sight, she'd never felt so alone.

Chapter Fourteen

"I'VE NEVER HEARD of this restaurant before," West said as he drove the engine down the twisty road that ran along the east side of Wildwood Lake. The sun was setting, casting a strange orange glow across the calm lake. There weren't any people hanging out along the shore, and no boats speeding across the water. The lake was almost eerily calm.

"It used to be called something else. Duke's maybe? Or Luke's?" Tori told him from the passenger seat. The rest of the firefighters were in the back cab. The coveted passenger seat was on a rotating schedule, Tori being the lucky one up tonight. Everyone fought over that damn passenger seat, which West found amusing. He'd done the same thing himself at the other stations he'd worked at.

"Ah, Duke's. I remember that place." It had always been too fancy for his family's blood. It was more of a tourist location, or where the kids would take their prom dates for dinner, though he'd never taken his there. Couldn't afford it. And after a while, he hadn't really cared.

"Yeah, well the building was sold and the new owners renovated the place over the winter," Tori yelled over the siren, which he'd just flicked on. They were driving through a more populated area and he wanted to offer up a warning that they were coming through. Sometimes the flashing lights weren't enough.

Not that they encountered much traffic. He could see the flume of smoke in the air up ahead, thick and black, indicating that a structure was burning, though it didn't look as intense as it had only a few minutes ago. He knew there was another engine already on scene and a couple of sheriff's deputies were there as well for crowd control.

He pressed the accelerator a little more firmly with his booted foot, eager to arrive. He didn't know much beyond that the top floor of the building, where the bar was, was on fire. He hoped like hell there weren't too many people inside and that they'd all gotten out safely, but it was high tourist season. Meaning big crowds flocked to the lakeside, renting cabins, camping, or holing up in the more expensive boutique hotels.

The town was overrun with tourists all summer long, right through the fall and until the first snow fell. Hell, even then businesses tried to appeal to visitors by turning Wildwood into a Christmas village. Wildwood lived and died by the tourist industry. If a brand-new restaurant burnt to the ground, that could hurt the town in the long run, though really the tourists would just find somewhere else to hang out.

West pulled the engine into the large parking lot of the restaurant—now called Wildwood BBQ & Bar, so original—shutting off the siren as he pulled up to the front, as close to the building as he could get, squeezing the engine in between an ambulance and a deputy car already parked there. His crew jumped out and started pulling off the hose while West went over to the other captain. He knew the guy's last name was Jefferson because that's all anyone ever called him.

"What's going on?" he asked.

"We have most of it under control," Jefferson said, his voice grim as he stared up at the building. "Your brother's here. Said there might be a few people still unaccounted for. He's checking right now."

"Shit." West rubbed his hand along his jaw, checking out the building as well. The restaurant was large, one of the closest to the lake, and currently the grassy area that surrounded the building was filled with people, the evacuated restaurant patrons most likely. The fire had been put out, but thin dark smoke still billowed out from the top floor's broken windows, the wood siding was black in spots, and the roof had mostly caved in. The bottom story appeared in relatively good shape, but water and smoke damage could make those extensive renovations pretty much obsolete.

"We need rescue. Stat. People are still inside." A familiar voice came from behind West and he whirled around to find Lane striding toward him, looking so upset West knew that whatever he was about to tell him was bad.

Real bad.

But he didn't give his brother a chance to explain. "We're going inside," he called to his crew as he started toward the front door without hesitation. Lane jogged along beside him, and West's crew fell into step behind them. His radio crackled at his hip but he ignored it, determination and fear making his heart race.

"Listen to me." Lane grabbed his arm, halting him at the top of the steps leading to the restaurant entry. His crew stopped just behind him, confusion on their faces as they waited. "They can't find Harper. They've looked everywhere, but she's nowhere to be found." Lane's words almost slurred he said them so fast.

West's heart felt like it shattered into a thousand tiny little pieces. "What do you mean they can't find Harper? Why was she here?" His heartbeat roared in his ears as he tried to focus on what Lane was saying. Something about Lane coming upon Wren outside and her panicking, crying that she hadn't seen Harper and she could still be in there. She hadn't seen Delilah either. He was thankful that Wren was okay. But…

"Wait a minute, Delilah *and* Harper could still be inside?" West didn't even hesitate. He barged through the front doors, Lane yelling at him to stop, commanding West's crew not to go inside.

His crew might've come to a halt, but West wouldn't listen, not that he was thinking much. No way could he stop. Harper was in there. He had to find her. What if she was trapped upstairs? God, what if she was hurt? Unconscious? Stuck in a smoke-filled room unable to breathe…

West shook the horrific thoughts out of his mind. He couldn't think like that. It would fuck him up royally when he needed to focus.

Adrenaline coursed through his veins as he paused, trying to assess the situation despite the panic clawing at his insides. Glancing around, he saw that the lower level looked pretty normal, with the exception of extensive smudges of black smoke on the white walls and the tables and chairs dripping with water. He scanned the room for the stairs, finding them tucked to the right side of the hostess station. West started up them just as Lane finally grabbed hold of his arm and stopped him.

"You can't go up there." Lane jerked him closer, gripping him tight. "I won't let you put your life at risk, damn it. The floor is damaged. If you can even manage to get your ass up there, you could fall right through."

"Fuck you," West said through clenched teeth. "I need to find her." He tried to pull out of Lane's grip, but it was no use. His fingers were clamped tight like a vise. "Let me go, asshole."

"No. She's not up there. No one's up there." Lane shook him, his expression determined, eyes serious. "Trust me. They're not inside."

"Then I need to find them." West swallowed hard, ignoring the panic racing through his blood. "Now."

HARPER HAD STUMBLED out of the restaurant, coughing as the smoke surrounded her, blocking her vision. She'd glanced around, grunting when people pushed past her, nearly knocking her to the ground, and she decided to follow them instead of working against them. She was missing one sandal and her bare foot hurt from when someone had stepped on her toes earlier.

But none of that mattered. She was out of the burning restaurant.

She was alive.

But she still couldn't find Delilah and Wren, had been wandering around for what felt like hours looking for them. She sniffed, realizing that she'd been crying, and she wiped at her eyes, brushed the tears off her cheeks. Now was not the time to fall apart like a baby. She needed to find her friends and make sure they were safe. Then they needed to get the hell out of here.

Panic filling her, she told herself to remain calm as she jogged around the side of the building, the grass soft and damp against her bare foot. People were everywhere, all of them scared, talking loudly, many of them crying. She heard the wail of sirens, the sound piercing and never seeming to let up. Clapping her hands over her ears, she stopped and glanced around, watching in quiet awe as a group of firefighters stood in a line and aimed a giant hose at one of the upper windows, the hard spray of water putting out the lingering flames. She wondered if West was here. He had to be. But where was he?

And no way could her friends still be up there…could they?

Deciding she was wasting time, she started running again, her gaze everywhere as she looked for Wren and Delilah. So many people milled about, the panic so thick she could practically see it. She coughed, the smoke still aggravating her lungs, and she stopped to rest, bending over to place her hands on her knees as she tried to catch her breath.

"Harper! Oh my God, there you are!"

She turned to find Delilah running toward her, her phone clutched in her hand. Her hair was a wreck, her face dirty, and her shirt was torn at the hem, but Harper had never seen a more beautiful sight.

"I was trying to call you," Delilah said as she yanked Harper into her arms and hugged her so tight she was afraid Delilah would crush a few bones. "I was so scared," she mumbled against her hair.

"Where's Wren? Have you seen her?" Harper asked, clutching Delilah close. The relief that flooded Harper made her bones wobbly. She was so glad to have found her friend.

Delilah pulled away, shaking her head. She grabbed hold of Harper's hand and started leading her back toward the building. "We need to go look for her. What if she's still inside?"

Harper glanced at the still-smoldering building. Worry made her stomach cramp, but she needed to stay calm. Wren was fine. She had to be. "We should stay here and watch for her." It killed her to say that, but she knew it was the right thing. They needed to stay in one place. If they started looking, they might miss their friend. "Did you try calling her?"

"Yes, but she didn't answer." Delilah's lower lip started to tremble and her eyes filled with tears. "She was so pissed at us and I was just as mad. Now I can't freaking find her. This is—" Delilah took a stuttering breath. "Not the way I wanted our last moments to be."

"Delilah, stop talking like that! She's fine." She couldn't let Delilah think along those lines. They needed to stay positive. She took in the fire engines and patrol cars in the parking lot, her heart easing just knowing who could possibly be nearby. "Have you seen Lane or West yet?"

"No." Delilah sniffed, tears sliding down her dirty cheeks and leaving visible tracks. "You're the first person I've found." She hauled Harper back into her arms, holding her close, and Harper let her.

"We'll be fine. We'll find her. Everything's going to be fine." She smoothed her hand over Delilah's hair, trying to soothe her.

Hoping like crazy that she was speaking the truth.

"COME ON, MAN. We'll find them. There's a large group of people out back by the dock. Maybe the girls are with them," Lane suggested, turning West around and leading him out of the building.

Misery settled low in his gut as he tried to put on a brave face and ordered his crew to start mopping up. All he could think about was Harper. What if the girls weren't there? Christ, he hadn't seen Harper in days. Hadn't held her, kissed her…

Regret slammed into him like a fist, making his stomach twist and churn. His job kept him away most of the time and he didn't mind. He usually preferred it because if he was working, at least he was doing something and getting paid. But now, thinking of Harper, how she could be hurt and he hadn't seen her in so long…

Fuck, he didn't know what he'd do if something had happened to her. He'd never forgive himself.

Without a word, they went outside and around to the back of the building, heading down toward the dock. Lane remained silent, and West was damn thankful.

He had to find Harper, see her with his own eyes, hold her in his arms. Once he found her, would he be able to let her go?

No.

The overwhelming realization didn't even faze him.

"Where's Wren?" he finally asked Lane as they drew closer to the dock.

"With Holden. He's on the other engine. You didn't see him?" Lane glanced in his direction.

West shook his head, increasing his pace. "How can you be so damn calm?" He felt like his nerves were doing a jig in his veins. His entire body was shaking, though he was doing his damnedest to appear otherwise.

"I'm just trying to do my job," Lane said quietly, his gaze everywhere as he took in all the people standing in small groups, huddled against each other as the temperature dropped along with the sun. Crickets chirped. The water lapped against the shore. Just another early summer night in Wildwood with the acrid scent of smoke in the air and the quiet sobs of panicked people whose lives had just flashed before their eyes.

Yeah. West wasn't usually prone to dramatics, but he was feeling pretty melodramatic at this particular moment. If he didn't find Harper soon…

"Lane!" The familiar sound of Delilah's voice had them both turning. There she was. Her dark hair was a wild tangle about her head, her face was smudged and her eyes were red and watery, but otherwise she was alive. "Oh my God!"

Delilah ran toward them but Lane was faster. He met her halfway and gathered Delilah into his arms, his mouth at her temple as he crushed her against him.

West felt a smidgen of relief, but it wasn't nearly enough. Where the hell was Harper?

"You're here."

West whirled around, his heart dropping to somewhere in the vicinity of his toes when he found Harper standing in front of him. Her white shirt was streaked and dirty and there was a bloody, angry scratch on her forehead, but otherwise she looked good.

She looked *alive*.

"I'm here," he croaked just before he pulled her into his arms and held her as close as he could get her. He tangled his fingers in her soft hair, pressing her face against his chest as he closed his eyes and breathed deep, saying a little prayer of thanks that he'd found her safe and sound. He wasn't a religious person, not by a long shot, but he was so grateful he couldn't help it. "God, Harper, it just about destroyed me when Lane said they couldn't find you."

"Is Wren okay?" she asked, pulling away slightly so she could look at him, her eyes welling up with tears.

"Yeah, baby. Wren's fine. She's out front with Holden." He smoothed his hand over her hair, pushing it away from her face. "Are *you* okay?"

She nodded, and then pressed her face against his chest once again. "I got separated from everyone. Wren and Delilah. They were all pushing and shoving to get out of there and I lost my shoe. Almost fell down the stairs, but I somehow got out. It was so scary." Her voice was muffled against his chest and he kissed her forehead, trying not to touch the scratch there. "I only just found Delilah a couple of minutes ago. I think she almost squeezed me to death when she hugged me."

That she was trying to make a joke during a time like this was sort of unbelievable. But people did strange things when they'd had a traumatic experience. He'd seen it firsthand time and again. "You need medical attention." West put his hands on her shoulders and pulled away so he could examine her carefully. "Are you hurt anywhere else?"

She shook her head. "I'm not hurt anywhere, West, I swear. I'm fine."

"You have a cut on your forehead." He stepped closer, examining it. It wasn't too deep, but it was ugly and would probably hurt once the adrenaline wore off. "I can take you back to the engine and look at it myself. There are ambulances on site too if you'd rather have an EMT take care of you."

"I'm fine." She threw herself at him, her arms coming around his waist, her face muffled against his chest once again. "I freaked out so bad, West. When I couldn't find the girls, I didn't know what to do. I was crying, thinking that was the last time I'd ever see them." She sniffed and he knew she was crying, which broke his hard-as-hell heart. He hadn't thought anyone could sneak past it, but somehow, Harper managed to. "Wren was so mad at me and Delilah right before it all happened. We got into a fight and we were leaving when the fire broke out."

"Wait a minute." He pulled her away from him again, staring into her eyes. "Why was Wren mad at you?"

Her expression instantly became guilt-ridden and she dropped her gaze. "I told her about…us."

He blinked. "She knows?"

Harper had asked him during one of their earlier phone conversations not to mention they were seeing each other to anyone else in the family besides Lane and he'd respected her wishes. Even though it ate him up inside, thinking she might be…what? Ashamed of him?

But now here she was telling Wren the truth. Could she want more from him? Could she actually want a real relationship? Being with her now, knowing that she was safe, made what they were doing seem more serious. More real. Though it had always been real with Harper. He was never just messing around with her.

"You know I'd been keeping it from her. I figured we both had our secrets and I thought I was okay with it. But it started to eat at me. I never keep secrets from Wren. She's my best friend and I didn't want her to find out what was going on from someone else. I felt I owed her an explanation, you know? That she needed to hear the truth from me."

"Okay," he said slowly, wondering why it was such a big deal to him. Yeah, he had his secrets, but he'd known that if he kept seeing Harper, eventually it would've gotten out anyway. And he'd expect their friends and family to be happy for them. Or so he'd hoped.

"She's always said how much she hated it when her friends became interested in her brothers. Girls used her just to get closer to you and Lane and even Holden," Harper explained.

He knew about it. Had dumped a couple of girls back in high school when they were dumb enough to tell him what they'd done to Wren. He would never let anyone treat his sister badly, especially a girl who was just trying to get with him. "So Wren knows about us, but she's not happy about it?"

Harper shrugged. "She didn't seem happy when I told her. Though for some reason she got even angrier at Delilah." She winced. "I told her that Delilah had a thing for Lane too. Delilah got mad at me."

"I doubt she's mad anymore." West looked over to where Lane still stood with Delilah. They were all wrapped up in each other too. They even looked like a couple, though he'd bet money Lane would deny he had feelings for Delilah. He was stubborn. Hell, all the Gallaghers were. Even Wren.

"You're not mad I told your sister, are you?" Harper's face crumpled. "I'm so sorry. I didn't mean to make such a mess of this. Now I've turned it into this big deal and it's so not."

"It's fine." He hugged her yet again, not able to stop himself from holding on to her, though her words still stung.

It wasn't a big deal to her? Why did hearing her say those words hurt so much? Is that how she really felt? Or was she just saying that? Only moments ago he'd thought she'd been truly hurt or…worse. Just the idea of her in pain had devastated him.

He didn't want to let her go. Fuck all that summer fling nonsense. He knew it was good between him and Harper. He wanted something real.

But did she?

"Listen, I know my timing is for shit, but I need to get back to work," he told her, hating the disappointment that crossed her pretty face. "Gotta check on my crew. I'm still on duty. I just—I had to make sure you were okay."

"I'm fine. Really." She bent her head, plucked at the front of his shirt. "I promise. I'm just glad to see you."

"I'm really fucking glad you're alive." He cupped her cheek, tilted her face up so her gaze met his. He skimmed his thumb across her skin, smudging the soot there. "You scared the shit out of me."

She smiled tremulously. "I was scared too."

He stroked her cheek again, wishing he could kiss her, but he didn't. There were people everywhere and he was, as he told her, on duty. "Come with me to the parking lot. I'll have someone check out your wound and bandage you up," he said, taking her hand.

HARPER LET WEST lead her back up to the parking lot of the restaurant, Delilah and Lane just behind them. Harper's nose wrinkled at the lingering smoke in the air. She was exhausted, her head hurt, and her eyes burned. But she was so incredibly glad her hand was in West's. He kept looking back at her, as if to reassure himself that she was with him, and she offered him a shy smile, wondering what could be possibly going through that mysterious brain of his.

She knew what was going through hers. Finding herself alone among the chaos, her friends nowhere in sight, she'd firmly believed something horrible had happened to Wren and Delilah.

Thank God they were all right.

And she was still shaky, her fingers trembling as West tightened his grip on them. She released a shuddery breath when West introduced her to the two EMTs who sat her down on the back end of the ambulance and started checking out her head wound. She didn't know when she got hurt, hadn't realized the cut was even there until West had pointed out.

"Luckily, you won't need stitches," the EMT said as she probed at the skin around the cut. She'd told Harper her name was Laura. "We can clean the wound up, put a butterfly bandage on it and you'll be good as new."

"Will it scar?" She didn't mean to sound vain, but she didn't want a big jagged scar slashed across her forehead.

"Somewhat but nothing major. The butterfly bandage should bring the skin close enough together to ensure it won't be a bad scar." Laura smiled, her gaze warm. Kind. "You're lucky you didn't get hurt worse."

"I don't even know how it happened." Harper winced when Laura started to dab ointment onto the wound. "Is everyone else okay? They found everyone, right?" She really hoped they did.

"Yes, everyone's been accounted for." Laura hesitated, studying Harper's forehead. "I heard it was crazy in there when the fire first broke out. So many people."

"Do they know how it happened?" When the EMT didn't say anything, Harper went on. "The fire?"

"I haven't heard anything mentioned yet about the cause. I'm sure they're investigating it."

"There you are." Wren rushed up, her expression one of pure relief, though she was just as dirty as they rest of them, all from the soot and smoke. Harper felt that same relief wash over her, leaving her weak. She'd known Wren was safe, but it felt good to see her with her own two eyes. "Weston said they'd found you, but I had to see it for myself."

"I'm okay," Harper said as Wren reached out and grabbed her hand, giving it a squeeze. "The bar doesn't look so good, but I'm fine. And you? West mentioned that you were with Holden."

"I'm okay too. It was scary though. Amazing how comforting my little brother can be when he's in job mode." Wren released her hand and stepped back as Laura continued to work on Harper. It was only when she was done and headed back into the ambulance to put away her supplies that Wren came and sat with Harper.

Harper took a deep, trembling breath, telling herself it was now or never. She needed to apologize and make things right again with her best friend. Despite the nearby EMTs and the people who were still milling about, she had to do it now.

"I'm sorry I wasn't honest with you about West," Harper said. "I know you're mad at me and I can understand why. I just, I didn't know what was really going on with West and me." She hung her head, looking down at the ground. "I still don't and I didn't want to make a big deal about it. I don't think he wanted me to make a big deal either."

"Well, now we all know so he's going to have to deal with the big deal." When Harper lifted her head, she found Wren was smiling at her. "Harper, I don't care if you're dating my brother. I care about you and worry that he might hurt you, but I just want you happy. And I want Weston happy too. He's not the easiest person to get along with—"

"He's changed," Harper interrupted, her heart suddenly feeling lighter. She hadn't realized how important Wren's approval was until she had it. "I really…care about him." Could see herself falling in love with him too, though she couldn't admit that to Wren. She could hardly admit it to herself. What had just happened between her and West had left a funny feeling inside her chest. He'd looked at her as if she meant the world to him, but was that true? Or was it just the life-or-death situation? "We have fun together. Though really, it's still very new."

"Just, be careful. He's not big on commitment." They both started to laugh. That was the understatement of the year. And hadn't one of them said that right before the fire broke out? "Though he's always had a soft spot for you," Wren added softly.

"Delilah said the same thing." Harper's smile faded. "You're not mad at Delilah, are you? What you said to her was pretty harsh."

Wren frowned. "I know. I need to apologize to her when this is all over. I was already mad about you seeing West and that you kept it from me. Then you hit me with the Delilah and Lane thing and I saw red. I said the first thing that came to mind and I knew it would hurt her."

"I think it hurt her pretty bad," Harper said quietly. "It was kind of a low blow."

"Yeah. I'm a jerk." Wren shook her head. "I don't know where she is right now, but West reassured me that he saw her and she's fine. I'll call her in the morning."

Harper decided it was best not to tell Wren that Delilah was off being comforted by Lane. They'd looked pretty cozy together, but that could've just been their reaction to a near-death experience. Lane rarely let any emotions show. He'd probably slip that mask right back on as soon as he was sure that Delilah was okay.

Just like West had done once he realized that she was all right. Going back into work mode, claiming he was on duty. He was, she knew that, but she didn't like how easily he'd walked away from her.

Harper frowned. Was it that easy for him? Could he really keep this thing between them casual when she couldn't? Most likely.

And that thought was the most disturbing one of all.

Chapter Fifteen

IT WAS JUST after eight in the morning when Lane stopped by the station to deliver the news.

"It was arson," Lane said grimly after he pulled West outside, away from the prying eyes and curious ears of his crew. Everyone else was in the kitchen, cleaning up after breakfast. Tate's engine had arrived late last night, everyone tired and dirty but relieved to be back on home turf. His crew was released and all went home, though Tate had stayed the night. He was in the garage now, checking over his engine like it was his precious baby.

Talk about a workaholic. He was worse than West, and that was saying something.

"No surprise." West had fully expected to hear this. There was no other explanation for what had happened upstairs at the Wildwood BBQ & Bar last night. Before the crews finished mopping up and the prevention team came by, West had already had his suspicions, along with everyone else. He'd heard the bartender's explanation and listened to a few witnesses explain what they saw.

More like what they *didn't* see.

From what West could figure, it had been a premeditated fire. But why? To hurt innocent people? Or just burn down a building? Was this some sort of statement? The damage could've been so much worse. Whoever had done this was lucky he or she wasn't facing murder charges.

"Was it linked to the other fires?" West asked.

Lane shrugged. "Not sure yet."

"Are we going to make this public?"

"We'll probably be forced to. There are already too many people curious to know what started this fire in the first place," Lane explained.

West would rather have the townspeople aware of what was going on than keep them in the dark. Going public with the news would be a great way to gather more information too. Someone might've seen something. "Should we get Tate into this discussion? He's in the garage checking over his engine."

"Yeah, we better tell him." Lane started to head over to the garage, but West stopped him with a hand on the shoulder, causing Lane to look back at him.

"I know now is probably not the right time, but can I ask you a personal question first?" When Lane nodded, West continued. "Tell me what's going on with you and Delilah."

Lane's expression shuttered, his gaze wary. He shrugged off West's hand. "Nothing at all. She's a friend. That's it."

"Bullshit. She's into you." There was no reason to play games or be vague. West may as well lay it all out on the line. "She likes you. I know she does. But you keep pushing her away."

"I'm not interested in Delilah. Not like that." Lane looked away, a muscle working in his jaw. A telltale sign that he was irritated. "We'd never work out anyway so what's the point?"

West frowned. "Why would you say that? If you like her and she likes you, I don't see how the two of you spending time together would be a problem."

"It's not that easy. We're totally different." Lane hesitated. "We want different things."

"What do you want anyway, Lane? To come home to an empty house every night and make a boring meal for one before you recline in your chair with a beer in your hand watching shitty reality TV? That sounds fucking awful if you ask me." West shook his head.

"Well, you should know, considering that's probably what you do every night when you're not working. Am I right?" The look Lane sent him was pointed.

Damn it, yeah he was. Though he wasn't a huge fan of reality TV. "Okay, you got me. But I'm seriously starting to think I don't want that life anymore." It was too damn lonely, not that he would admit that to his coldhearted big brother.

After what happened last night, when he thought he lost Harper, he couldn't stop thinking about her. Lost sleep over her, tossing and turning all night once he finally slipped into bed. He'd been so damn tempted to call her first thing this morning but then thought it better to let her rest and recover.

Besides, what could he do? He was still stuck at the station. He felt fucking helpless.

Lane raised his brows. "Really? You better make sure you mean that before you go spouting off to Harper that you're all in or whatever other bullshit you're going to feed her. You don't want to break her heart, do you?"

West was taken aback at Lane's words. "I won't break her heart." Then he thought of what she'd said last night, how they were just having fun. Messing around. That it wasn't anything serious, what they were doing. "She just got out of a relationship. I won't be the heartbreaker, Roger already did that."

"Actually, *she* dumped Roger. Though he agreed pretty readily that their relationship wasn't working." Well, well, well, look at his brother, the gossipmonger. Who knew Lane had it in him? "Don't forget that. And she's had a thing for you for *years*. Back when she was nothing but a kid with a harmless crush. Well, I'm guessing what she feels for you now is a lot more than that. I'd bet money that you could snap her heart clean in half if you said or did the wrong thing. Trust me on this, little brother." Lane patted his shoulder. "Be careful with that girl. She's delicate. And she's totally into you."

West had nothing to say to his brother's speech. He only nodded as they walked over to the garage side by side. They spoke to Tate, and Lane ran through the grim details of what the fire investigation had turned up so far. Tate had plenty to say about it, most of his comments heavily peppered with expletives, but West remained silent. He was too distracted, mulling over what Lane had said about Harper.

Was she really too delicate? Did he have the power to break her heart? Ever since they started in on this...relationship, this seeing-each-other type thing, he'd felt like *she* was the dangerous one. How comfortable he felt with her, her easygoing personality. With her sweet smiles and soft sighs, those pretty, delicious lips and that luscious body. The way she'd murmured his name just before he entered her...

Yeah. She could strike pure terror in the most calloused of hearts, and his was one of the hardest. She made him want to feel. Worse, she made him want more. More time with Harper, more of those conversations they shared, those sweet smiles and soft sighs, her delicious lips and her luscious body. He liked the way she looked at him, like he was in on their private joke and they were the only ones who knew the punch line...

But the thing that terrified him the most? That they might not be on the same page after all. Did they want the same things? What the hell did he really want anyway? Was he thinking too fast, getting too ahead of himself?

Probably.

Being honest with Harper, laying everything out on the line, should be his next move. He wanted to be open. He wanted to tell her the truth, to tell her what he wanted. But that would be pretty damn tough, especially when he wasn't exactly sure what he wanted himself.

He knew one thing though. What had happened last night, the close call with Harper, how he'd thought at one point that he could possibly lose her…it had made him realize that she needed to know how he *really* felt about her. And he needed to tell her.

As soon as he possibly could.

HARPER ACHED EVERYWHERE. She hadn't bothered going in to work at the diner, hadn't bothered getting out of bed. Once she got home last night, her grandma had taken care of her, fed her chicken soup in bed after she'd taken a shower and washed off all the dirt and grime.

She'd slept in, then taken another hot shower to ease the tenderness in her sore muscles, careful not to get the bandage on her forehead wet. She'd fixed herself a bagel with cream cheese and then crawled back into bed when she discovered she could barely keep her eyes open. Played around on her phone for a little while, texted Wren and Delilah, checking in on them, before falling back asleep.

It wasn't until her grandma came home in the early evening that she woke up again.

"Lazy bones," her grandma chastised as she entered the bedroom and flicked on the overhead light. Harper blinked, threw her arm over her eyes to block the brightness. "Are you not well? Do you need to see a doctor?"

"I'm fine. Just tired," Harper grumbled. "Turn off the light, please."

"Hmm." Grandma did as she asked then bustled into the room and pulled the blinds open instead, letting in the waning sunlight. "Tell me the truth, young lady. Is your head okay? Are you traumatized by what happened to you yesterday? Do you need counseling? I could arrange it, you know."

Leave it to her grandma to be blunt. "No, I'm all right. Really. I'm just…" She didn't know what she was. Tired and achy, yes, that was legitimate. Scared of the unknown because she hadn't heard from West all day…?

There was that too.

Wren and Delilah, she was good with. They'd said their apologies and were back to normal. It wouldn't be weird between them because they'd known each other far too long to let it get weird. But West?

They'd seen each other briefly before she left with the girls. He'd hugged her, kissed her cheek, and whispered that he'd contact her tomorrow. Well, tomorrow was almost gone with no word from West. She knew he was busy. He was working and hadn't been off duty for days. The man was exhausted and most likely had more important things to do.

It still hurt though, that she hadn't heard from him. She'd sent him a quick text but no reply so far. She didn't know what to think anymore. Did she matter? Would she ever matter? Wasn't she worth a two-word text? Even a one-word text would've sufficed. At least that would've shown that he was thinking about her.

But he couldn't even manage that and it hurt. The man turned her into a thousand neuroses, all of them rising to the surface and making her an agitated, dysfunctional mess. When it came to Weston Gallagher, she cared too damn much.

That could totally end up biting her in the butt.

"You're just what?" her grandma asked, interrupting her panic-induced thoughts.

"I'm just…" Harper shrugged. "Quietly freaking out over my life choices?"

"Oh dear." Grandma settled heavily on the edge of the mattress, wearing a frown of concern. "What exactly are you talking about?"

Taking a deep breath, Harper decided to just go for it. She unloaded completely on her grandmother, from her worry over breaking up with Roger to seeing West a few times—though she left out the sex details—to her fear that she was working a nowhere job—*no offense, Grandma*—and she felt like she was making one major mistake after the next.

"See, that's the beauty of it all," Grandma said when she finally stopped rambling. "You're young. You're allowed to make mistakes. They're a part of life."

"But I'm twenty-six," Harper reminded her. "Aren't I too old for this sort of thing?" She worried that she was. Her mom and dad had been married by the time they were twenty-six. And Harper had been on the marriage track with Roger…until she wasn't. Now she had a sometimes-boyfriend who kissed like a dream but was a total commitment-phobe.

"You're never too old to make a mistake. Trust me." Grandma laughed and shook her head. "I still make mistakes all the time."

"You do?" Harper could hardly believe it. She knew it was silly, but her grandma had always been pretty much perfect in her eyes.

"Oh yes, constantly. I date the wrong sort of men. I've made a mess of my business filing and organization and now my granddaughter has to work extra hard to set me straight."

Harper smiled a little at that.

"I worry about the diner. Should I sell it? Should I keep it open? Is it worth the hassle? I worry about money. Do I have enough? I worry about my friends. I get mad when that old broad Martha Burlingame makes those snide remarks and tries to tear me down. I despise that woman." She shook her head. "I still miss your grandpa, though I don't like to say that out loud. My son—your father—makes me crazy, but I know he means well. Yes, I make mistakes, but I'm a grown woman, a human being, and I'm allowed. Just like you, dear."

Harper nodded, dropping her gaze to the comforter. She plucked at an imaginary string, taking in what her grandma said. "I feel like I should have it all together."

"No one has it all together. Not really. Just because they act perfect or have the perfect job or the perfect-looking boyfriend or husband or whatever, no one is perfect. We're all struggling, all trying to live our lives as best we can. Just make sure you're having fun, because if we're not having any fun, then what's the point?" Grandma smiled. "Now. That nice boy you've been seeing is coming over tonight. I saw him earlier at the diner and told him to come pick you up and take you out."

"Wait, what?" Harper sat up straighter in bed, running her hand over her tangled hair. "Who are you talking about?" She knew exactly who Grandma was talking about, but she needed to hear her say his name.

"Why, Weston Gallagher of course. He came by earlier this morning for a second breakfast after they released him at the station. Was hoping he'd see you, but I told him you were home resting."

He came by the BFD to *see* her? Never before had Harper been tempted to hit her grandma. Until now. "You told him that?" she squeaked. Her grandma should've called her immediately to let her know West stopped by.

"Well, yes. Every girl needs her beauty sleep before she goes on a date with her handsome boyfriend. And that Weston is drop-dead gorgeous, dear, especially in that uniform he wears. You sure know how to pick 'em." Grandma fanned herself with her hand.

Harper burst out laughing. "He is pretty cute, huh?" Oh, he was so cute. And sweet. And sexy. And funny.

She could go on and on.

"That's putting it mildly. Now. Go. Get ready. He'll be here in an hour."

"You really arranged a time for him to come by and everything?" Harper gaped at her.

"Of course, I did. I told him not to disturb you during the day, so that's why you never heard from him. Poor boy is probably champing at the bit to see you. Which truly, that's the ideal situation." The smile on her grandma's face was downright naughty.

Harper leaned forward and pulled her grandma into her arms, squeezing her tight. "Thank you," she murmured. "For the pep talk. And for arranging my date tonight."

"Anytime, dear. Though you really should consider looking for a new place to live eventually. Or else I'm afraid we'll start cramping each other's style," Grandma said with a laugh.

Chapter Sixteen

THE DOORBELL RANG, and Harper counted to ten before answering it, as per her grandma's instructions.

"Anticipation is key, darling," she'd trilled as she left the house to go on her own date for the evening. "And don't expect me back until tomorrow morning!"

Harper could've done without that little detail.

Running her hands down the front of her dress, she shook her hair behind her shoulders, took a deep breath, and slowly opened the door.

West stood on the doorstep, clad in jeans and a black T-shirt, a bouquet of wildflowers clutched in his hand. His eyes went wide upon first seeing her, scanning the entire length of her body. "Hey."

She smiled. "Hi."

He took a step forward, thrusting the flowers toward her. "These are for you."

"They're beautiful, thank you." She took the bouquet from him and brought the flowers to her nose, inhaling deeply their sweet scent. "Come in, let me put these in water."

He followed her inside, shutting the door behind him as she went into the kitchen. She was nervous, having him so close, so many unspoken things shimmering between them. She wanted to grab him. Kiss him. Tell him she missed him, but she was still feeling a little unsure.

So instead, she grabbed a vase from the cupboard and filled it with water, then arranged the flowers carefully, her fingers drifting over the soft, colorful petals. She could feel West enter the kitchen, his magnetic presence making her shiver, and she went completely still. She was trying to come up with something to say when he was suddenly behind her, his big hands engulfing her hips, his warm mouth close to her ear.

"It about killed me to follow your grandma's orders today," he murmured, his lips brushing against her neck and sending tingles scattering all over her skin.

She placed her hands over his when he slid his arms around her waist. "What were her orders?"

"Don't contact you. No texting, no calling, no nothing. Just show up here at seven and take you out. Bring flowers." He paused. "That's exactly what she told me to do."

Aw, her grandma was the best. Though it had been a slow form of torture, not hearing from West all day. "Why didn't you just give in and call me?" She leaned against him, loving how his solid, lean body cradled hers.

"She said it would be better this way. I think her exact words were *anticipation is key.*" He kissed her neck again, his lips lingering. "I think she might've been right."

Harper absolutely couldn't take it anymore. She turned, slipped her arms around his neck, and rose up on tiptoe, pressing her mouth to his. West immediately cupped the back of her head with one hand, keeping her there, not that he had to. His mouth devoured hers and he tilted his head to the side, taking the kiss deeper in an instant. She moaned at the first touch of his tongue against hers, overwhelmed by the way he took total command of the situation.

"Is your grandma here?" he asked a few long, delicious minutes later, his lips brushing against hers as he spoke. He'd gathered the skirt of her sundress in his fingers until her butt was practically exposed and *now* he thought to ask if her grandma was around? "I'm about to throw you on the kitchen floor and get you naked if I don't watch it."

A thrill shivered down her spine at his dark words. "She's gone for the night."

He smiled, his fingers pulling the skirt higher, cool air hitting her backside. She tried to swat his hand away, but he was too quick. "So are you saying I can get you naked in your grandma's guest room? Or is that too crazy?"

It wasn't too crazy. She was just as eager to have him. She withdrew from his arms and took his hand, smiling as she led him back to her temporary bedroom. "Come with me."

He rushed her into the small room, slamming the door behind him and gathering her into his arms. She went willingly, laughing when he fell onto the bed with her. He rolled over so that she was pinned beneath him, his knees bracketing her hips, his hands pressed on either side of her head.

"I probably should've done the right thing and taken you to dinner first," he said, his gaze roaming over her face as he studied her. "But I couldn't wait. It's been too long since we've been alone. Really alone."

She was rendered breathless by his admission. "I'm glad you couldn't wait."

West bent down and kissed her, his lips lingering, warm and soft. "I've missed you."

"I've missed you too."

"I want you."

Harper smiled, tilting her head back when he slid his lips down the length of her neck. She closed her eyes, losing herself in the delicious sensation of his mouth on her skin. "I want you too."

"I think I'm falling in love with you."

She went completely still as all the air lodged in her throat. Her eyes popped open and she stared up at the ceiling. His admission threw her for a complete loop. Could he really mean it? West wasn't one to just toss out careless declarations. She knew this. But still...

He lifted his head, his somber gaze meeting hers. "I meant what I said, Harper. After what happened yesterday, it made me realize just how much I care about you. You've always been a part of my life, and I took that for granted. I was a jerk to you in the past and I regret it so damn much. I came back here to Wildwood, and you should've treated me like shit for leaving you like I did, but you didn't. Not really. And somehow, you allowed me back into your life, and you worked your way into my heart."

She reached for his face, drifted her fingers along his smooth-shaven jaw. "You've always been in my heart, West. For years, you've been there, even when you shouldn't have been."

Closing his eyes, he leaned into her palm. "I know, and I took advantage of that when I kissed you that one night. But no more. You deserve to know how I feel about you."

"And how do you feel about me?" She dropped her hand from his face, her chest squeezing tight as she waited for his answer.

"Like I said, I'm falling in love with you." She parted her lips to speak but he cut her off, resting his fingers on her mouth. "I realize we haven't been seeing each other long, but we've known each other for years. What we have is special, Harper. And I'm not willing to let it go."

"I don't want to let you go either." She kissed the tips of his fingers before he lifted them away from her mouth and replaced them with his lips. The kiss was deep, hot, his tongue tangling with hers as he pressed her into the mattress. She slid her hands beneath his shirt, running her fingernails up and down the smooth expanse of his back as he growled against her lips, making her giggle.

"That feels good. I've missed having your hands on me," he murmured, impatiently tugging at her skirt. "I want you naked."

She laughed. "Impatient much?"

"For you, hell yes. I haven't touched you like this in weeks." He lifted away from her and tugged the dress up so it was bunched around her waist, exposing her pale green cotton panties to his gaze. He groaned when he first spotted them. "Christ, you're trying to kill me."

"They're not that sexy," she protested, gasping when he shifted so that his mouth was on her belly, his warm lips on sensitive skin, making her shiver.

"Everything you wear is sexy. You're sexy." He curled his fingers around the waistband of her panties and tugged them off, his movements erratic. He ran his mouth greedily over her skin, along her thighs, her hot throbbing core. Her hipbones, her stomach, her breasts…as if he was trying his best to consume her, though his mouth never lingered long. Growls of impatience escaped him and she was just as eager, kicking off her underwear, lifting her arms when he pulled the dress up over her head and tossed it on the floor. She wore no bra so she was completely naked, earning an appreciative glance from West before he straight up attacked her.

Oh, and she reveled in it. He was like a man possessed. His hands were everywhere, all over her body, caressing her breasts, slipping between her legs, testing how wet she was for him. She writhed beneath his touch, her fingers fumbling over the button of his jeans, pulling at them impatiently. She wanted them off. She wanted him just as naked as she was and within moments, like magic, he was.

He rolled on the condom that he had stashed in his jeans and wasted no time pushing inside her, burying himself so deeply that all she could do was close her eyes and clutch him close. There was no finesse, no prolonging the orgasm or drawing out the act. It was just pure, ani-malistic…fucking. A word she'd never used to describe any of the times she'd had sex before.

With West, she loved it. He was completely out of con-trol, his mouth locked with hers as his hips shifted, his cock thrusting inside her again and again and again…

Until all she could see were stars.

"I'M A SELFISH jackass," West said as soon as he could find his voice once again. He held Harper close in his arms, her warm, naked body wrapped all around his, their legs tangled up together. They were limp and sated, his eyes closed and his brain buzzing, feeling completely wiped out in the best possible way. He pressed his mouth to her forehead, trying to calm his breathing. His dick twitched, letting him know it was up for round two.

Un-freaking-believable.

Harper made this low murmuring sound in her throat, sexy as hell as she shifted against him, her hand brushing against his belly, his cock, making it spring magically back to life. "Why do you say that?"

"I was completely out of control just now." Almost embarrassingly so. It had been too long since he had her and he'd just wanted her so damn much, he couldn't hold back. He'd fully planned on making love to her. Nice and slow, his mouth all over her body, hands mapping her skin. Learning every little spot that drove her out of her mind, discovering her intimate secrets.

But no. He'd tried that approach and gave up fast. Instead, he'd rutted on her like some sort of wild caveman, coming with a shout after five minutes of being inside her. It was sort of embarrassing.

"I thought it was hot." She tilted her head back, smiling up at him. "It felt like you really wanted me."

Her fingers brushed against his stomach again, making him flinch. "That's the truth. I always really want you. And now that we got that out of the way, I'll make sure to take my time with you the next go-round."

"There's going to be a next go-round?" She sounded so hopeful he couldn't help but smile.

"There are going to be lots of go-rounds." He kissed her, mentally reminding himself to go slow. "If I have it my way, we won't leave this bed tonight."

"That sounds nice." A dreamy sigh escaped her and she snuggled closer, her mouth on his shoulder. "What about dinner?"

"I'm sure we'll figure something out eventually." Currently he only wanted to feast on her.

He held her close, loving how easily she curled her naked body around his. For the first time in a long time, he felt…content. It definitely had to do with the woman in his arms, but he also knew it had to do with being back home. In Wildwood. Once a town he couldn't wait to get away from, he was happy here. He liked where he worked. He enjoyed spending time with his siblings. His relationship with his father was permanently damaged, but with time, maybe it would get easier. He didn't mind the gossip, and the familiarity that came with returning to his hometown.

More than anything, he cared about the woman lying beside him, her hair in his face, her arm slung around his middle like she owned him. It felt good, having someone, having somewhere he belonged.

It felt right.

"What about the future for us, West?" She gazed up at him, nibbling on her lower lip. She looked unsure, hesitant. "You probably don't want to talk about the heavy stuff right now, but I have to ask. What do you want for…us?"

He brushed a wild tangle of hair away from her face, his fingers skimming her cheeks as his gaze never left hers. She had the prettiest eyes. She had the prettiest everything. Why had he never seen it before? When they were younger and she'd followed him around like a lovesick puppy…what an idiot he'd been. "I want to be with you. Only you. And we'll just need to take it day by day, okay? This summer, I'm going to be busy with work. It's going to get crazier, I know it. There's a lot going on around here. The fire season is going to be intense, what with the drought conditions and the…" He thought of the arsonist. He didn't want to scare her, but it was happening. Hell, they were talking about it in the local newspaper. "The possible arsonist. I might be gone for weeks at a time. That's the norm during a busy fire season."

She nodded, her eyes full of sadness. "I understand."

"But I'll always be thinking about you, even when we're not together. You're mine, Harper. And I'm yours." He leaned in and kissed her, taking it deep, leaving her breathless. "Nothing's going to change that."

"Okay," she whispered, her lips moving against his as she spoke. "I can deal with that."

"Yeah?" He smiled and she smiled in return.

"Yeah." She kissed him this time, her sweet lips molding to his. "I feel like my every dream has come true."

"Me too, baby." He splayed his hand across her back. "Me too."

Epilogue

"YOU'RE SO HAPPY you're glowing." Delilah made a face and shook her head, her nose wrinkling. "It's kind of disgusting."

"Oh stop, Delilah. You're just jealous," Wren added, nudging Delilah with her elbow before she flashed a smile in Harper's direction. "I can admit that I'm a teeny bit jealous too, but we're happy for you and West. Really."

"She's right. We are," Delilah added softly.

They were at the Bigfoot Diner, eating lunch. Harper's grandma was their server and she brought out the biggest burgers the three women had ever seen, along with a red plastic basket heaped with French fries. She'd informed them, "Eat. You girls are too skinny," and then scooted back to the kitchen.

So they did.

Harper couldn't help but beam like a crazy woman at her friends. She was deliriously happy. The man of her dreams had become the man of her reality. They'd been serious for only a month, if that. They were on the accelerated plan—West had called it a few weeks ago, wearing that sexy, panty-melting grin of his.

Dipping her head, Harper smiled to herself. Yes, every time West flashed her that knowing smile, her panties melted. Her heart melted, her resolve melted…he knew just how to affect her. Giving her the right look, touching her in the right way, whispering the right words…

A shiver moved down her spine just thinking about him.

"Uh-oh, she's in a West-induced stupor again," Wren said, her tone teasing. "Seems to be happening a lot lately."

Harper lifted her head, laughing. "I can't help it if I'm happy."

Delilah took a sip from her soda. "We love that you're happy. I don't remember you smiling this much when you were with Roger."

Her smile faded. She still felt a little guilty about Roger, for how quickly she'd broken it off with him and ended up with West. He was always polite when she ran into him around town, which was often. She'd heard a few rumors that he'd gone on some dates, though they didn't seem to be anything serious. He didn't seem to be pining away for her, which was a huge relief…

"How's it going here?" Wren asked, her question knocking Harper out of her thoughts. "Still deeply entrenched in the training program?"

Harper rolled her eyes, grabbing a fry and popping it into her mouth. The salty goodness was almost too much.

Funny how she spent so much time at the BFD yet never grew tired of the delicious food. "Grandma loves to boss me around like I'm in the military when I'm here, but we both know she's a big old softy."

A softy who was becoming increasingly dependent on her granddaughter to eventually run the business side of the diner. Harper had cleaned out the office by the end of her self-imposed two-week deadline. She'd then proceeded to reorganize everything and, with her grandma's permission, bought a new computer along with the best accounting software she could find.

She'd taken over the financial records, the accounts payable and receivable...all of it.

"You're going to be running this place one day," Delilah said as she glanced around the busy diner. "Do you think she's going to retire soon?"

"Doubtful." Harper's grandma loved the BFD too much to retire—yet.

"I never talk to my brother anymore so I have to find out everything through you." Wren lowered her voice. "Tell us what's up with the fire situation."

The low grumbles among the townspeople were getting louder, and Cal Fire had recently released official information—there was definitely an arsonist in their area. The biggest damage so far had been to the restaurant, but other fires had been started since then, all of them vegetation fires that hadn't burned much beyond a few acres. An investigative team was called in and Lane, along with the rest of the sheriff's department, was working with them in tandem. West had mentioned a few details to her, but he was pretty mum about the entire subject.

Harper understood. Some things he couldn't really discuss. Besides, when they were together, they didn't really talk about work…

"I don't know much," Harper offered with a little shrug. "They're all on the job."

"Lane isn't saying much either," Wren said, making Delilah laugh.

"When does Lane ever say much?" she asked sarcastically.

True that.

"So when are you two crazy kids going to move in together?" Wren asked Harper, changing the subject.

Harper's mouth dropped open. Was Wren a mind reader or what? "We were just discussing that a few nights ago," she admitted softly.

They'd been tangled up in bed, the sheet kicked off onto the floor, Harper half draped across West's limp-with-pleasure body. He'd skimmed his fingers down her back, given her a light smack on her butt, and murmured, "You should move in with me."

She'd protested, made all the right noises because *come on*. They couldn't live together so fast. But West wouldn't take no for an answer. And now she was trying to work up the courage to tell her family that she was moving in with her new boyfriend so quickly after moving out of her old boyfriend's house.

Yeah. The gossipmongers of Wildwood were going to have a field day with this one. But maybe it wouldn't be so awful. West was the beloved bad boy who was now doing good. And Harper had always been Wildwood's good girl—who'd suddenly gone a little bad.

And being bad with West had never felt so good.

"So you're moving in with him?" Delilah asked, her eyebrows rising. "That's so great!"

"Shh, we haven't officially confirmed it yet," Harper said, hoping no one was paying any attention to the three of them. "But yes, it's going to happen. Soon."

Both Wren and Delilah looked like they were bouncing in their seats. It was sort of ridiculous. And silly—silly enough that Harper couldn't help but burst out laughing. She'd never felt so loved before. By her friends, her family.

By West.

The front door of the BFD swung open and in walked a Cal Fire crew, West taking up the rear. His hair was a little wild—it was time for a haircut—and there was a dark smudge on his cheek from God knew what. But wow, did he look good in his uniform, that beloved easy smile on his face as he nodded at the waitress who began to lead the fire crew to a table.

He scanned the room, looking for Harper, of that she was sure, and she lifted her hand in an acknowledging wave, her heart swelling near to bursting at seeing him. He said something to the rest of his crew and made his way to Harper's table, smiling at all three women when he stopped in front of their table.

"Ladies." He nodded at Delilah and Wren before his head swiveled in her direction, that knowing smile that got her every single time curling his perfect lips. "Harper."

"What are you doing here?" She sounded breathless. Could feel her friends watching her like she was put on this earth to amuse them, but damn it, she couldn't help herself. Her boyfriend made her feel fluttery inside each time he looked at her.

"We just finished up a call and we're starving. Thought we'd stop at the BFD." He gave her a look, one that said *I've seen you naked.*

Harper blushed. "It's good to see you," she murmured, making his smile grow.

They didn't say anything, just smiled at each other until finally Delilah made an irritated noise.

"You two need to get a room," she muttered.

"Ew, that's my brother you're talking about," Wren practically squealed.

Ignoring them both, West's gaze never left Harper's. "Come with me," he said, his voice low.

Without hesitation Harper slid out of the booth and followed him to the back of the diner, where he opened the supply closet door and pulled her inside. The moment the door shut, he had his hands on her, his mouth fused with hers. It was so dark that she kicked the mop bucket when she took a step back, making them both laugh softly when the mop handle clattered to the floor.

"We need to stop meeting like this," he whispered, his mouth hot as he kissed her neck, making her shiver.

"You're the one who always wants to have a rendez-vous in the supply closet when you stop by," she reminded him, sighing when he nibbled on her ear.

"I never hear you protest." He lifted his head and she knew he was watching her, even though he couldn't see much since it was so dark. "I've missed you."

"You're off shift tomorrow."

"Yeah." He pulled her in for a hug, holding her close. "But I don't like being away from you."

This coming from the man who loved his job. His confession made her feel warm and fuzzy inside. "Hasn't any of your crew figured out what you're doing when you keep stopping by the BFD?"

"They've got me all figured out. Not like we're hiding it." He slipped his hand beneath her chin and tilted her face up, his mouth mere inches from her. "They know I can't get enough of you."

Before she could answer him, West kissed her breathless, his lips, his tongue, his hands busy. Long, kiss-filled minutes later, she finally pulled away from him, running a hand over her hair, smoothing her shirt back into place. "We should go back out."

He huffed out a frustrated breath. "You're right."

"You need to order lunch."

"They know what I want."

"You should make sure they're okay."

"They're fine." His hands were back on her again, slipping beneath the hem of her T-shirt and touching her bare skin.

"What if you get another call?" She sounded breathless again. How did he do this to her every time he kissed her?

"I have the radio attached to my belt, babe." He went in for another kiss, but she stopped him, her hands braced on his chest. "You worry too much."

"You're right," she whispered against his lips as she slid her hands up over his shoulders. "I do."

"Stop worrying and kiss me."

Harper did as he requested.

No questions asked.

Acknowledgments

I HAVE TO acknowledge my grandma when it comes to this book. No, she doesn't own a restaurant called the Bigfoot Diner (though that would be awesome), but she is pretty cool and very independent. My grandpa died when I was fourteen. My grandparents lived out in the country far from any town, and my grandma couldn't drive. She was so dependent on my grandpa for everything. But after he died, she realized she needed to get busy learning how to drive so my stepdad taught her. She bought a tiny Honda Civic and I remember driving around with her—I was probably fifteen?—and another car cut her off. She flipped him the bird and called him a dirty word. I was *shocked*. This was my grandma! A sweet little old lady who never cursed and definitely never pointed her middle finger at anyone!

But now I realize as I've grown older that hey, my grandma was pretty young when her husband died—in her early fifties. And once enough mourning time had passed, the vultures started circling. Meaning, the old men in the senior community in her small town, the widowers and divorced guys, who were looking for a new mate in their golden years. One of them was named…

Buster Boner.

I kid you not! When my grandma told me his name, I couldn't stop laughing. I went with her to a friend's house one summer and actually met him. He was very old and very interested in my grandma. He called her out of the blue one day and told her, "Grace, I have seventy thousand dollars in the bank and two tickets to Hawaii. Are you with me?" She said no. I asked her why (I mean, I met him and could see why she said no, but hey! That's some decent money and Hawaii!) and she said, "He's nothing but an old coot." He eventually found someone else to take to Hawaii. I vaguely remember an article in her local newspaper that claimed Buster Boner was missing! His children hadn't heard from him in days and it turned out he'd gone out of town with a lady friend (that's what my grandma called her). Guess he found someone to spend all his money with after all.

Buster Boner is long gone, but his name lives on. I told my grandma a few days ago that I wrote him into this story, and the first words out of her mouth were, "Oh, that old coot? I haven't thought of him in forever!" She still calls him that. She cracks me up. I love my grandma. She also said I just forever immortalized Buster Boner and I told her how could I forget a name like that? Real life is definitely stranger than fiction.

I also have to mention my husband because he's the one who came up with the Bigfoot Diner idea and told me I could call it the BFD. In a mountain town near us there used to be a Bigfoot-themed restaurant and as a kid, he loved going to that place. Though his idea was really his opening up an actual restaurant like that. I squashed that plan and told him I'd create a fictional restaurant instead. So the BFD is for him.

Want more from the boys of Wildwood?

Keep reading for a sneak peek from

SMOLDER

Coming Summer 2016 from Avon Impulse.

DELILAH MADE HER way down the hall before she turned to glare at Lane, her eyes glowing in the dim light. "I swear to God, you're the most ignorant person I've ever met in my life. Do you do that on purpose or what?"

"Do I do what on purpose?" He scratched at the center of his chest, hating how his heart still beat erratically. So hard it felt like it was going to bust right through his ribcage.

They stared at each other for a long, quiet moment. He could hear the muffled voices coming from outside, the kitchen door slamming. Most likely it was Wren making her way to the backyard. He hoped like hell she wouldn't spread rumors about what she just saw.

Knowing his sister, she'd probably tell Harper. And West. And anyone else with ears who could hear her talk. She had a big enough mouth.

"You make me insane," Delilah finally said, her voice…sad? Well, hell, he didn't expect that. Irritation, yes. That was the name of their game. But upsetting her? Making her sad? Making her look so damn…hopeless?

He didn't like that. At all. But what could he say? What could he do to make it better? He was an expert at his job. Could handle any tough situation thrown at him. But when it came to women—this particular woman—he was as clueless as a newborn baby.

"Figures you'd have no reply," she muttered. With a roll of her eyes and a flick of her ponytail, she started to walk away but he caught up with her in three long strides, grasping hold of her slender arm so she couldn't escape. She glanced over her shoulder at him, those big brown eyes wide and full of so many questions. Questions he wasn't prepared to answer.

"I'm sorry," he murmured, his voice low, his stomach doing weird flip-flops when her gaze dropped to his mouth and seemed to linger there. The electric buzz was still there, sizzling between them, pinging between their bodies, and he felt as if every hair on his body was standing on end.

"You say that a lot, you know." She sighed and carefully disentangled her arm from his hold. He immediately missed touching her. "It doesn't have to be this difficult."

She was right. He fought the attraction they had for each other constantly. "I don't know if you understand what exactly I'm struggling with…"

"I think you struggle with the same thing I do, you're just not brave enough to go for it." She stared him down but he refused to flinch. Delilah basically just called him a coward. And that hurt. "I don't know much more obvious I need to be."

"Dee—" he started, but she reached toward him, her fingers settling on his parted lips, that tiny, seemingly innocent touch searing him to his very soul. But there was nothing innocent about Delilah. Not when it came to the two of them together. She knew just how her touch affected him. And he knew he had the same effect on her.

She lifted her gaze to his once more. "You know we want each other."

His entire body went stiff. Especially his dick.

"You know I'll do whatever you want, whenever you want," she continued. "Wherever you want me," she murmured, her voice full of so much fucking promise his mouth went dry as every dirty word and thought seemed to clog his throat. Never had she talked to him like this before.

"You don't know what you're saying," he practically choked out. She couldn't know what her words did to him. If she kept this up she'd tear down every one of his defenses and he'd finally give in.

He frowned. That didn't sound like a bad idea.

"I know exactly what I'm saying." She licked her lips, her lids growing heavy, reminding him of some sultry seductress you only saw in the movies or on television. "The ball is in your court. Your move, Lane."

And with that she left, leaving behind a cloud of her intoxicating perfume.

About the Author

USA Today bestselling author **KAREN ERICKSON** writes what she loves to read—sexy contemporary romance. Published since 2006, she's a native Californian who lives in the foothills below Yosemite with her husband and three children. She also writes as *NYT* and *USA Today* bestselling author Monica Murphy. You can find her at www.karenerickson.com.

Discover great authors, exclusive offers, and more at hc.com.

Give in to your Impulses . . .
Continue reading for excerpts from
our newest Avon Impulse books.
Available now wherever e-books are sold.

HARD EVER AFTER
A HARD INK NOVELLA
By Laura Kaye

WILD AT HEART
By T.J. Kline

THE BRIDE WORE STARLIGHT
A SEVEN BRIDES FOR SEVEN COWBOYS NOVEL
By Lizbeth Selvig

An Excerpt from

HARD EVER AFTER
A Hard Ink Novella
By Laura Kaye

After a long battle to discover the truth, the men
and women of Hard Ink have a lot to celebrate,
especially the wedding of two of their own—
Nick Rixey and Becca Merritt—whose hard-
fought love deserves a happy ending. As Nick and
the team shift from crisis mode to building their
new security consulting firm, Becca heads back to
work at the ER. But amid the everyday chaos of
their demanding jobs and upcoming nuptials, an
old menace they thought was long gone reemerges,
threatening the peace they've only just found.

Wearing only her bra and jeans, Becca sat in a chair in the middle of Nick's tattoo room. Since the shop was closed while Jeremy focused on getting the construction on the other half of the building started, they were the only ones down there. The driving beat of a rock song played from the radio as Nick moved around the room getting everything ready.

Cabinets and a long counter filled one wall, which was otherwise decorated with drawings, tattoo designs, posters, and photographs of clients.

Becca had seen Nick work before and loved the dichotomy of this hard-edged, lethal soldier having a soft, artistic side. He was really freaking talented, too.

He handed her three sheets of paper. "I worked up a couple different fonts. What do you think?"

She shifted between the pages. "This one," she said, settling on the cursive design that best interweaved the letters in the words *Only, Always, Forever*.

"That was my favorite, too," he said, giving her a wink. "How is this for size? Bigger? Smaller?"

The total design as he had it on the sheet was about four inches square, the words stacked atop one another. "This looks good to me. What do you think?"

Nick nodded and came behind her. He folded the sheet to focus on the design, then held it against the back of her right shoulder. "Yeah. This is a good size for the space. Gonna be fucking beautiful." He leaned down and pressed a kiss to her skin. "Let me go make the stencil, and we're ready to go."

A few minutes later, he cleaned her skin, affixed the stencil, and let her look at its placement before getting her settled into the chair again.

He pulled her bra strap off to the side. "Ready?"

"Very," she said, butterflies doing a small loop in her belly.

The tattoo machine came to life on a low buzz. "Just relax and let me know if you need a break, okay?" he said, dipping the tip into a little plastic cup of black ink.

"Okay." His gloved hands fell against her skin, and then the needles. Almost a scratching feeling, it didn't hurt nearly as bad as she thought it would. And just like when he'd drawn on her with skin markers, she was already dying to see what it looked like.

"How you doing?" he asked in a voice full of concentration she found utterly sexy. Just the thought that he was permanently altering her skin—just like he'd permanently altered her heart, her life, her very soul—sent a hot thrill through her blood.

"I'm good," she said, relaxing into the sensation of the bite moving across her skin. "Is it weird that I kinda like how it feels?"

He didn't answer right away as the needle moved in a long line. He pulled the machine away and wiped at her shoulder. "Not weird at all," he said, his voice a little gravelly. "Some people like the sensation and even find getting tattoos addictive."

"I can see that," she said. He worked without talking for a stretch, and the combination of the quiet intensity radiating off of him, the driving rock beat, and the buzz of the machine was heady and intoxicating. She found herself breathing a little faster and wanting so much more of him to be touching so much more of her. If she thought he was sexy putting ink on someone else, it was nothing compared to how she felt when he was doing it to her.

"What are you thinking about so hard?" Nick asked, his breath caressing her bare shoulder.

"Really want to know?" she asked, already smiling at what his reaction might be.

"Always," he said, wiping at her skin. He dipped the machine in the ink and leaned in again.

"How turned on this is making me." She really wanted to turn to see his expression but knew she wasn't supposed to move.

He pulled the machine away again. "Jesus, Becca. You're killing me here."

She grinned. "I asked if you really wanted to know."

An Excerpt from

WILD AT HEART
By T.J. Kline

Bailey Hart has never felt at home in her small
town. So when her band gets their big break
in Los Angeles, "Wild Hart" can't run fast
enough . . . If only there weren't so many reasons
to stay. After a harrowing stint in the Oakland
Police Department, Chase McKee has returned
home a hero, and yet he feels anything but. And
when he finds out Bailey might be leaving for
good, the feelings he's always harbored for his
best friend's cousin just won't stay hidden.

Chase picked up on the roar of the engine long before the motorcycle actually came into view. Reaching for the radar gun, he aimed it in the direction of the sound.

Ninety-two miles per hour. Did this guy have a death wish?

He'd no more tapped the gas on the cruiser when the motorcycle blazed past him in a midnight-blue streak. He flipped on his lights and siren and the bike immediately slowed as the rider glanced backward before pulling onto the shoulder.

At least he has some respect for the law, he thought acerbically as he stopped behind the motorcycle and ran the plates.

The registered owner's name came up on his computer screen and his eyes shot back to the rider.

"Damn it," he muttered, rolling his shoulders back and preparing for the battle he had no doubt was coming. Chase rolled his eyes and climbed out of the vehicle with a sigh of resignation. Crossing his arms, he greeted the most beautiful woman—and the biggest troublemaker—he'd ever met as she slid her helmet off her head and brushed stray hairs back into her low honey-colored ponytail.

"Funny seeing you here, Bailey. When did you get this thing, and are you trying to kill yourself with it?"

She turned her dazzling pearly whites on him, her blue

eyes flashing with mischief as she set the helmet on the seat behind her. Chase had been dying to ask her out ever since his return to town almost two years ago but she had no idea and, unfortunately, he needed to keep it that way. Her cousin Justin was one of his best friends, and if he knew Chase thought of Bailey as anything other than Justin's "little sister," Chase would probably have to arrest his friend for assaulting a police officer. Not to mention that he'd need to check himself into the hospital.

"Just picked it up last week." Her fingers ran lovingly over the blue gas tank between her thighs, and he felt his body immediately react. He stifled the response. "I guess I'm still getting used to how much power it has."

"Ya think?" He couldn't help but chuckle at her understatement as he clicked the top of his pen and started writing out a speeding ticket. "I need your license and registration."

"Aw, come on, Chase. Really?" She bit her lower lip, looking up at him from under her thick, dark lashes, and he felt the heat of desire trickle down his chest and center low in his belly. "I'll slow down. I swear."

"And you'll never do it again, right?" He didn't believe her for a second. Everyone knew Bailey's reputation as the wild child of the Hart family. She didn't just march to the beat of her own drum, she conducted the entire orchestra to a tune of her design.

"You know, you should come by for dinner tonight. I'm fixing enchiladas for them. We're hoping the spicy food will put Jules into labor. There'll be plenty if you want to stop by."

A flirtatious smile spread over her full lips and her eyes sparkled like sapphires. Chase felt the sizzle of heat come to life again. If he didn't know her better, he'd think she was flirting. That was the last thing he needed right now. He turned the pad toward her and handed her the pen, indicating she should sign the line. She stared up at him expectantly, practically batting her eyelashes.

Chase cocked his head to the side and gave her a lopsided grin. "Plying me with dinner isn't going to get you out of a ticket, Bailey."

Her eyes narrowed as he tapped the pad again. Bailey jerked it from his hand and scribbled her name, slapping the pen against it irritably when she finished. He ripped her copy of the citation from the pad and handed it back to her with the other documents. "You *do* realize trying to bribe an officer is a felony, right?"

She cocked a brow at him as she slid her helmet back over her head and slipped her sunglasses on, starting the engine. "Who said anything about bribing you? Maybe I was trying to poison you."

Chase couldn't help but laugh as she eased the bike back onto the road. "Murder One is a felony, too," he yelled after her.

Damn, that woman could turn him on faster than she did that bike.

An Excerpt from

THE BRIDE WORE STARLIGHT
A Seven Brides for Seven Cowboys Novel
By Lizbeth Selvig

Once comfortable on stage in front of thousands, Joely Crockett is now mortified at the thought of walking—or rolling—down the aisle at her sisters' wedding. Scarred and wheelchair-bound, the former beauty queen has lost more than the ability to walk—she's lost her fire. But when one handsome, arrogant guest accuses her of milking her injuries and ignites her ire, Joely finally starts to feel truly alive again, and soon it's impossible for her to resist her heart's desire.

"You look lost."

She started at an unexpected, masculine voice and swung her gaze to the dining room doorway. Her mouth went dry as a summer drought, and her pulse hiccupped before it began to race. The man who stood there with a hot smile and a confident demeanor owned a pair of the sharpest hazel eyes she'd ever seen, sandy-gold hair the color of a palomino stallion, and a jaw and cheekbones strong enough to have been chiseled out of Wyoming granite. Most unsettling of all was a smile that likely could have charmed Sunday school teachers out of their knickers—in any era past or present.

After she'd stared for an impolite number of seconds, Joely lowered her eyes and cupped her chin so her thumb rode up the left side of her in order to hide the scar. She'd convinced herself it made her look thoughtful and masked the self-consciousness she'd never suffered before the accident.

"I might be lost," she said. "But I'm probably not."

"You're Joellen."

"Not unless you're angry at me."

He raised one amused brow. "I'm not."

"Then it's Joely."

"I admit it; I knew that. What I don't know is how a pretty

little thing like you could possibly be sitting all alone like this in a house full of women."

She stared, not sure whether she was annoyed at the "pretty little thing" epithet or surprised at his mind-reading ability, since she'd been wondering the same thing.

"My whole family is in the kitchen through that door. I could ask you the same thing. What's a patronizing cowboy like you doing in my mother's dining room knowing my name when I don't know yours?"

The grin widened, and he strode into the room, dark denim jeans fitted nicely on his hips, a subtle plaid shirt tucked at the waist, and a casual brown sport coat giving him a touch of western class. He reached her in three strides, his cowboy boot heels beating a soft, pleasant cadence on the oak floor. "Alec Morrissey," he said, holding out his hand. "Alexander if you're mad at me."

The name left her stunned again. She knew it. Anyone who followed rodeo knew it. But he couldn't be *the* Alec Morrissey— the one who'd won three PRCA titles and then dropped out of sight half a dozen years ago . . . She shook her head to clear it before she could blurt a question that would sound stupid. She kept her hand over her scar by pretending to scratch her temple and took his hand to shake it. His firm, dry masculine grip sent a small warning shiver through her stomach.

"I'm not," she said.

"Not what?"

"Not mad at you."

"Ah. Even if I'm patronizing? Or if I admit I'm not a real cowboy? Which I'm not, by the way. I wear the boots because they're comfortable."

She wanted to tell him she'd only forgive him if he promised never to call her a pretty little thing again. Her father had called her that, but not in a proud papa kind of way. It had been more a "you're my delicate little flower, don't worry your pretty little head over such things" kind of way. But based on the confidence this man exuded, Joely doubted she could tell him to do or not do anything.

"Well, I can't lie. I'm disappointed about the cowboy part. But if you swear to quit being patronizing, I won't be mad."

He pulled out a chair beside her and sat backward on it, comfortable and easy, looking as if he'd lied about not being a cowboy and straddled seats and saddles every day.

"Ma'am, if calling you pretty is patronizing, I can't swear because any promise I made I would break every time I saw you."